Ranger showed the same determination as earlier.

The K-9's face was tilted downward, his nose inches from the debris beneath him, head moving side to side as he pawed at the building remains.

Deputy Rutherford drew in a sharp breath. "He found something, right? Isn't that what that means?"

"That's exactly what it means," Zack replied. He gave Ranger lots of encouragement as the K-9 continued to dig through the rubble. Was Lauren down there? He hoped they'd find her.

The deputy bent over, calling into the debris again. Judging from his demeanor, he didn't get a response. Zack looked behind him. The clouds that had dumped so much rain earlier were piled up on the western horizon. The sun was behind them. In two or three hours, it would be dark. If they couldn't get to Lauren soon, would the men keep working?

Rutherford straightened suddenly. "I got a response. It's weak, but I definitely heard 'Help...'"

Carol J. Post writes fun and fast-paced inspirational romantic suspense stories and lives in the beautiful mountains of North Carolina. She plays the piano and also enjoys sailing, hiking and camping—almost anything outdoors. Her daughters and grandkids live too far away for her liking, so she now pours all that nurturing into taking care of two highly spoiled black cats.

Books by Carol J. Post

Love Inspired Suspense

Shattered Haven
Hidden Identity
Mistletoe Justice
Buried Memories
Reunited by Danger
Fatal Recall
Lethal Legacy
Bodyguard for Christmas
Dangerous Relations
Trailing a Killer
Detecting Deadly Threats

Canine Defense

Searching for Evidence
Sniffing Out Justice
Uncovering the Truth

Visit the Author Profile page at LoveInspired.com for more titles.

DETECTING DEADLY THREATS

CAROL J. POST

LOVE INSPIRED SUSPENSE
INSPIRATIONAL ROMANCE

 **LOVE INSPIRED® SUSPENSE**
INSPIRATIONAL ROMANCE

Recycling programs
for this product may
not exist in your area.

ISBN-13: 978-1-335-90643-4

Detecting Deadly Threats

Love Inspired
22 Adelaide St. West, 41st Floor
Toronto, Ontario M5H 4E3, Canada
www.LoveInspired.com

HarperCollins Publishers
Macken House, 39/40 Mayor Street Upper,
Dublin 1, D01 C9W8, Ireland
www.HarperCollins.com

Printed in U.S.A.

God is our refuge and strength,
a very present help in trouble.
—*Psalm* 46:1

Thank you to my wonderful sister, Kim Coker—
my plotting partner, my research buddy
and my all-time best friend. You're the best sis ever!

Thank you to my editor, Katie Gowrie,
and my critique partners, Karen Fleming and
Sabrina Jarema. Your amazing insight
always makes my writing better.

And lastly, thank you to my husband, Chris,
for your love, encouragement and support.
You're the inspiration for every hero I write.

ONE

A vibration passed through the ground beneath Lauren Hollander's feet.

She paused, letting her Canon 35-millimeter camera dangle from its strap around her neck. What she'd felt was similar to the vibration created with a heavy truck passing by.

But there weren't any trucks in the area.

She glanced around. No one else seemed to have noticed. Early afternoon on a Tuesday, only a couple handfuls of people wandered the park.

She shrugged and raised her camera again. Having grown up in Ridgely, Tennessee, she was no stranger to earthquakes—the idea of them, if not the actual experience. The New Madrid was the most active seismic zone east of the Rocky Mountains. She'd learned all about it in school.

But ninth grade was a long time ago. And during her almost thirty years, she could count on one hand the number of quakes that had been strong enough to feel.

A pair of blue jays flew toward the fountain

at the other end of the small park. She aimed the camera and adjusted the settings for a longer view. A little boy stood on the short wall that surrounded the fountain, his mother's arms around him. Trees formed a striking backdrop to the scene with their vibrant displays of orange and yellow and red.

As Lauren moved closer, sounds of childish laughter reached her. She snapped several pictures, walking in a wide arc until she could capture the little boy's face. Once satisfied, she removed the lens, slid it into its compartment in her bag and put away the camera. She'd already eaten her sandwich and apple and had thrown away the trash. Now her lunch break was over. Not that she couldn't extend it if she wanted to. She was the boss.

She crossed the street that ran between the park and her jewelry store as a familiar Buick LeSabre pulled into a parking space along the roadside. Although the late-October morning had started out chilly, the sun had warmed everything nicely. Now gray clouds were overtaking that sunshine.

Jerry Beckham stepped from the LeSabre and hurried toward the front landing. "Let me get the door for you, young lady."

Instead of reaching for the handle, she waited under the mansard with its gold letters identifying the establishment as Holland's Custom Jewelers.

When Dave Holland retired a year ago and agreed to carry the mortgage for her to buy the store, she hadn't bothered to change the name. *Holland* was close enough to *Hollander*. Even the "custom" part of the name fit, thanks to Dave's willingness to teach her every part of the business.

Jerry opened the door and glanced up at the sky. "Looks like we're gonna get rain."

"We need it." She led him inside and circled around behind the display cabinet where Abby, the store's part-time help, waited.

Abby handed her a sheet torn from the message pad. "The Whitmers' twenty-fifth anniversary is coming up, and Jack wants you to create a custom necklace for Kathryn."

"Awesome." Designing and creating pieces to customers' specifications was what she enjoyed the most, next to the personal interactions with people she'd known all her life. The joys of living in a small town.

"I'll leave you to it." Abby stepped from behind the counter. On her way to the door, she passed the old man with a greeting and pat on the shoulder. Tuesdays and Fridays were her half days. The schedule worked well with her college classes and kept Lauren from having to pay a full-time salary.

After setting her camera bag on the small table against the wall, she moved to the counter and pushed a porcelain plate toward Jerry. While she'd been at the park, Abby had restocked it. "Here, have a muffin."

A smile lit his face, deepening the creases at the corners of his eyes and mouth. Making two dozen mini muffins had been part of her morning routine for the past several years.

Jerry took a bite and rested a forearm on the glass surface. "Are you staying busy?"

"Just the usual. Last weekend, I took my girls camping."

Her "girls" were the six regular attendees of her church's Kids Club, third through sixth grade. She loved that age group. Actually, she loved kids, period, had always thought she'd have several of her own. Sometimes life threw unexpected curveballs.

Jerry nodded. "Sounds like fun, although I'm about fifty years past the age of wanting to chase kids around." He grew serious. "How's that brother of yours doing?"

He asked the question about once a month. It was more about her welfare than her brother's.

"Lyle's doing well." After his last prison term, he'd finally gotten his act together and become a productive member of society. "Still has his job at Precision Auto Repair."

Jerry nodded. "He's been there, what, five months?"

"Six." That was a record for him. Nine months out of jail was a record, too.

"He still living with you?"

"Nope. Got an apartment in town three weeks ago."

She could have gotten him out of her house sooner if she'd floated him a loan for the first month's rent and security deposit. Knowing she'd never see the money again, she'd opted to make him pay her room and board and put back half of his paycheck every week until he had enough to make it on his own.

"Good. I hated to see him taking advantage of you."

"Trust me, he didn't. He had chores and a whole bucketload of rules to follow." One of those rules was that he had to be home by 9:00 p.m., unless he got approval from her. The closest he'd ever come to complaining was once saying he was the only twenty-six-year-old guy in the state with a curfew.

She continued. "That supervision and stability was what he needed. So was getting him away from Memphis."

The day he'd turned eighteen, Lyle had hightailed it out of Ridgely to live it up in the big city. Worst decision ever. Not that he hadn't been in trouble before. But the people he'd gotten hooked up with in the city had made the troublemakers of Ridgely look like choirboys.

"I hope you're right."

His tone held more doubt than hope. He wasn't the only one who'd expressed concern. But she hadn't gone into this blind. Her brother was an expert at conning people. This time he actually seemed sincere.

"Getting almost beaten to death was a turning point for him." A group of inmates had jumped him. She'd gone to see him a week later and hardly recognized him. "He says he's really changed."

Jerry frowned. "You've heard that before."

Yeah, she had, at least a dozen times. "It's different this time. That experience scared him straight. He just needed a chance to make a fresh start, away from all the negative influences. I couldn't turn my back on him."

"He's not your responsibility anymore."

No, technically, he wasn't. But old habits were hard to break, and she couldn't stop feeling that she, in fact, *was* her brother's keeper.

She tilted her head to one side. "What's bringing this on?" He'd always been concerned about her helping Lyle, but now he seemed outright worried.

"I don't know." He frowned, and his gaze dipped to the floor. Yeah, he did know. He just didn't want to say anything.

"Tell me."

He heaved a sigh. "I was going into Family

Dollar last night as he was leaving. He had a busted lip and some bruises on his face. When I asked him what happened, he said he fell, hit his face on a railing."

A knot of uneasiness settled in her stomach. When she'd seen Lyle two days ago, he'd been fine. Had he gotten involved with men running drugs again and double-crossed them? Or had his past activities followed him from Memphis?

He shrugged. "Maybe that's what really happened. But be careful. I don't want you to get hurt."

"I'm keeping my eyes open." Time for a change in subject. "What have you been up to since I saw you last?"

"I planted some fall annuals in Ethel's window boxes." He shook his head, sadness filling his gray-blue eyes. "That woman sure loved her flowers."

Lauren rested a hand on his forearm. "I know you miss her."

After a few more minutes of chitchat, Jerry pushed himself away from the counter. "Well, I have a doctor's appointment. Gotta keep this ol' ticker going."

She looked out the front window. The sky was even darker now. "You'll have to hurry if you're going to beat the rain."

She watched him walk out and head toward the gray Buick. He'd been a regular customer for years, buying a small piece for every major and minor holiday. Several months ago, he'd lost his Ethel after fifty-three years of marriage. No longer a regular customer, he was now just a regular visitor. Some said he came for the muffins. Lauren knew better. He came for the conversation, that sense of connecting with another caring human being.

That was okay. The store wasn't just her livelihood. It was her life. It paid the bills, but it also satisfied her need to nurture and care for others. She could almost convince herself that it made a good substitute for the family she'd never have.

Lauren eased into a chair at the small table against the wall and pulled her camera from its bag. The laptop sitting there still had the cable connected. She plugged the other end into the port on her camera. With a few mouse clicks, the photos she'd taken began uploading to the cloud. While her computer did its thing, she turned back the cover on the spiral-bound notebook that lay in the middle of the table.

Yesterday, she'd met with a man who lived in nearby Tiptonville. He'd wanted a necklace designed for his wife, something that incorporated her love of music with her love for her children. After meeting with Jack Whitmer this afternoon, she'd likely have another piece to design.

She picked up a pencil and began to sketch. Maybe a wavy staff with three half notes, their heads made up by the birthstones of each of her children. The necklace was to be a Christmas gift, so she had almost two months to design something the customer liked and create the piece.

After sketching some other ideas, she raised both arms overhead in a stretch and shifted her gaze to the front window. The rain had come. It was now blowing against the glass, running down in sheets. She hoped Jerry had made it inside his doctor's office before the sky had opened up.

She stood and twisted side to side before walking around the counter to look out the front window. If the rain continued, she wouldn't have any more customers today. Someone would have to be desperate to venture out in this.

As she watched, a figure passed in front of the window. He was hunched over, face tilted downward, umbrella held so low it rested against the back of his head. Moments later, he swung open the door and stepped inside. Water dripped from his rain jacket, puddling on her hardwood floor.

"Can I help you?"

Without moving the umbrella or lifting his head, he turned slowly toward her, reaching under the yellow rain slicker. A sense of unease swept through her, and she took two steps back. In one smooth motion, he raised his head and swept aside the umbrella. A knit ski mask covered his face and hair. The next moment, she was staring down the barrel of a pistol.

Her heart stuttered, then pounded out a frenzied rhythm. What was she supposed to do? She'd never been held up before, hadn't even considered it in the safe, little town of Ridgely.

"You can have all my money." She moved toward the end of the counter, ready to circle behind and empty the cash register. Would it be enough to satisfy him? Most of her customers paid with credit cards. A small handful wrote checks.

"Stop!" The sharp tone brought her to an instant halt. "I don't want your money."

She turned to face him. "Jewelry?"

God, please let him be here for the jewelry. Because the other possibility was more frightening—that whoever had roughed up her brother had come to exact retribution on her, too.

He closed the distance between them in three swift steps. The next moment, he wrapped her upper arm in a viselike grip. She was right. He hadn't come to rob her. He'd come to hurt her.

"What do you want? I'll give you anything here." She gave her arm a tug in an attempt to move toward the counter.

His grip tightened more, sending needlelike pulses down her arm and into her fingers. "You're coming with me."

Her brain shut down. She couldn't move. For several moments, she forgot to breathe.

God, please send someone. She hesitated. *No,*

don't! Anyone who walked into the store would likely end up dead. If Lyle was the reason the man was here, this was her battle and hers alone. Jerry was right. She should never have brought him home.

The man pulled her toward the door. She resisted with all of her strength. He hardly seemed to notice. Though he was only two or three inches taller than her five-foot-five, he was at least double her weight.

She couldn't let him drag her out of there without a fight.

She tightened her left hand into a fist. Biting him or kneeing him in the groin was out of the question. She wasn't in position to do either. She swung toward his face with all the speed and strength she could muster. He turned his head, making it a grazing blow.

He released a string of expletives and slung her to the floor. She landed hard on her back. Her lungs seized for several agonizing moments. Before she could recover, his booted foot connected hard with her side. Pain, ragged and sharp, wrapped its talons around her ribcage, driving an involuntary scream from her throat.

As he jerked her to her feet, the roar of the deluge outside filled the space. Someone had opened the door.

Her chest clenched. "Don't come in! Call the police!"

The masked man spun in that direction, hauling her with him. The visitor stood in the open doorway. Lauren blinked several times. As expected, he was wearing a rain slicker and carrying an umbrella. He was also wearing a ski mask and holding a gun.

Two of them? No way would she make it out of this alive.

"Let her go." The raspy command came from the doorway.

Her assailant tightened his grip on her arm. "You take orders from us, not the other way around."

"I'm following your orders. I'm getting what I came for." The words held a thick accent, one she couldn't place. "This isn't part of the deal. Leave her alone."

"Get out of our way."

The foreigner moved fully inside, letting the door shut behind him. "I'll step aside for you, but you're not taking her."

Seconds ticked by as the two men stared each other down, each with his pistol trained on the other. Her captor jerked her in front of him. The same moment, a deafening crack pierced the semisilence. A sustained high-pitched ring started somewhere inside her head, pushing the muffled sound of the storm even farther away. The man with the accent clutched his side and dropped to his knees, groaning. He flopped to the side and rolled onto his back, legs drawn up.

The man who'd shot him hadn't intended to kill him. At that distance, he could have hit him center mass with his eyes closed. Maybe he was teaching him a lesson while also sending a message to her.

Pulling her toward the door, he tried to slide the wounded man out of their way. When that didn't work, he kicked him in the ribs. "Move it."

The moans morphed to a squeal before toning back down. Regardless of where he'd been shot, he was losing blood fast and wouldn't survive if he didn't get help soon. Blood had soaked through his T-shirt and was pooling on the floor beside him. No matter how he was threatened, he wasn't going to rise and crawl out of their way.

A small seed of hope sprouted. To move the injured man, her captor would have to release her. She glanced around. She'd never make it through the lobby and behind the counter without him shooting her in the back. Dashing out the front door wasn't an option, either. But her alarm panel was only three feet away. Two sideways steps would put her within easy reach. He wouldn't know what she had planned until it was too late.

He gave her a firm shake. "If you move, you'll end up like your would-be protector."

She gave a sharp nod. His gaze flicked past her toward the counter. His eyes widened almost imperceptibly. What had he seen? Before she could ponder it further, he released her. When he bent over to grasp the wounded man by the arm, she crept toward the keypad. He gave him a tug. When she pressed the first number of the panic code, a beep sounded. The man stiffened. By the time he spun around, she had all four digits entered. A shrill squeal filled the space.

Without looking to see his reaction, she sprinted toward the counter. As she dove over its top, another shot rang out. Glass shattered. A second later, she hit the floor with a thud. The alarm continued its shrill squeal, setting her teeth on edge. The system was monitored, but the police would never get there in time.

Before she could scramble into the back room, the same vibration she'd felt in the park rippled through the floor. But it was much stronger. And it didn't stop. Instead, it intensified.

More glass shattered. It was farther away than the counter, likely the front window. Walls begin to sway, and the building groaned. The sharp crack of spitting wood joined the crash of breaking glass. When she pushed herself to her feet, jagged pieces of the display cabinet had fallen onto the jewelry arranged inside. The wounded man lay two or three feet from the door. Her assailant was gone.

Creaks and groans surrounded her, building to a deafening roar, as if the building was in agony. She stumbled toward the back room, arms stretched out to the sides. If she could make it there and unlock the door, she could run to safety.

As the ground continued to shake, she lurched sideways, slamming her shoulder into the wall. Sharp, high-pitched creaks echoed above her. The ceiling was going to cave in, and with it, the entire apartment above. She couldn't make it. She dove under the table where she'd sat earlier.

The crash she'd expected came, ear-splitting and terrifying beyond anything she'd ever experienced. Studs, floor joists and drywall piled up around her. The table's metal legs buckled. Pain jolted her as one of them jabbed into her back, right below her rib cage. The table collapsed, pressing her body into the floor.

Her ears rang and her pulse went into overdrive. She couldn't breathe. She was going to suffocate.

She struggled in a tiny breath, and her throat closed up, rebelling against the dust and other particles she'd tried to take in. An involuntary cough followed. She tried to shift position, but she couldn't move. Every part of her body was pinned. Panic exploded inside.

She willed it to subside, forcing her chest and throat muscles to relax. She sucked in a slow, shallow breath, the sound a tight, painful squeak. Each breath that followed was a little easier.

The shaking had stopped. It was over. For now,

anyway. What she'd felt at the park had been a foreshock. There were sure to be aftershocks, causing the weight pressing down on her to shift and maybe increase, crushing her.

No, she wouldn't think about the what-ifs. She'd take it an hour at a time. Minute by minute, if she had to.

She'd survived. Someone would find her and get her out. People would know to look for her here. This was where she always was, every day except Sunday. She just had to hang on until rescue crews could get to her. Depending on the level of devastation, that could be as late as tomorrow, even the day after that.

Rainwater dripped in around her, seeping into her clothes. When the sun went down, the temperature would drop, and she'd be trapped in her dank, dark prison.

She prepared herself for hours of misery. Wet and cold. Without food and water. Chest too compressed to manage more than rapid, shallow breaths. A deep, agonizing ache in her back that felt more like organ than muscle or bone.

Waiting for rescue would test every bit of her endurance.

If she survived at all.

Zachery Kimball tapped the steering wheel with his thumbs in a rapid rhythm. Ahead of him, vehicles were at a dead standstill, sitting bumper to bumper. The view in his mirrors was similar. It looked as if everyone in Ridgely had a kid to pick up from Lara Kendall Elementary.

He'd been at his new job at R&K Metal Processing when the shaking had started. Like many of his coworkers, he had a home and family to check on. Home was a second-story apartment above a jewelry store. Family was his thirteen-year-old nephew. He'd acquired the nephew two months ago, the apartment just last week.

The nephew was safe. Zack had called the school before leaving work. He had the number programmed in his phone. Until this afternoon, he hadn't had to use it. What was amazing, though, was that the *school* hadn't yet called *him*. Of course, William had been there only two days. Even *he* couldn't get into trouble that quickly.

Over the next twenty minutes, vehicles crept forward in a start-and-stop pattern. As Zack drew closer to his destination, he looked over at the brick-and-stucco building with its green awnings, the words "Lara Kindall Elementary" above the double doors. He smiled. When William had learned that the school housed grades three through eight, he'd insisted that at thirteen, he was too cool to go to school with snotty-nosed third graders. Zack had advised him to bring it up at the next school board meeting, that he was sure the district would be happy to start a school just for the "cool" thirteen-year-olds. Sometimes, it was easy to be patient with the boy since he'd lost his mother. Other times, it wasn't. It all depended on how close Zack was to the end of his rope.

Finally, he was third in line for pickup. The rain had stopped. William stood talking with another boy who looked to be the same age. When he saw the red Mustang, he waved to his friend and strolled toward Zack. At least the kid thought his car was cool. So far, that was the only thing he'd done right.

William slung his pack into the back seat before sliding into the front. He didn't look too shaken up. In fact, he almost looked happy. Maybe he was excited about getting out of school early.

"You doing all right?"

"I'm cool."

"How bad was it?"

"Things started shaking. The teacher made us get under our desks. A window even busted out. It was *lit*."

Lit? Apparently that was a good thing. Zack pulled away from the school, shaking his head. This was the first time since they'd left LA that William hadn't been pouting or outright angry, much of it directed at Zack. He'd been at a loss as to what to do for him. Even counseling hadn't helped. Leave it to William to need a natural disaster to knock the chip off his shoulder.

"Are we going home?"

"After we pick up Ranger."

That had been his second call. Both his search and rescue dog and Jackie, the sitter, were fine. Once he picked up Ranger and checked his own place, he'd see if the dog's skills could be used anywhere. The structures he'd passed had sustained varying amounts of damage. Two were completely destroyed, jagged roof sections sitting awkwardly on tangled jumbles of wood, plaster, electrical wire and plumbing. They'd both been older wood-framed homes.

The other structures seemed to have fared better. That would be comforting, except the building that housed his apartment, with Holland's Custom Jewelers below, had to be close to a hundred years old.

The events of this afternoon still seemed surreal. He wasn't in California anymore but had just experienced an earthquake. In Tennessee. How was that even possible?

When he pulled into Jackie's driveway, she was sitting in the swing beneath the huge oak in her front yard. The black-and-tan coonhound lay at her feet. She approached Zack and passed off the leash. "I've already walked him, so he's ready to go."

"Thanks. I'll be leaving him home with my nephew for a while. The school sustained minor damage, and classes are canceled until they have inspections done." That was what they'd said

when he'd called, along with promising to no-
tify parents when classes resumed.

Zack unclipped Ranger's leash and let him
jump into the back. Then he headed toward his
apartment, a short distance north of town. As he
left the burg behind, his chest tightened. Flashing red and blue lit up the road in the distance,
somewhere close to his apartment.

He drew closer, and his heart sank. The jewelry store and his apartment above were gone. He
stared at the pile of debris, a lead weight filling
his gut. He'd sold almost all his possessions before leaving LA, so everything he and William
owned was in that mess.

He pulled off the road behind the Lake County
Sheriff's Office cruiser and looked through his
driver's-side window. What about his landlord
downstairs? Had she made it out of the building,
or was she trapped inside? He'd talked to her only
a handful of times, twice on the phone inquiring
about her ad for an apartment to rent and nailing
down the details, and once for her to give him
the key after he arrived. The other two times had
been even more brief—a wave and "good morning" as she'd opened her store while he'd walked
Ranger. Lauren's sweet spirit had instantly drawn
him to her, and he'd looked forward to getting
better acquainted with her.

"Where are we gonna live?" William's voice
came from beside him—weak, all attitude stripped

away. His jaw was slack, his eyebrows drawn together.

The boy's forlorn expression beat Zack down even further. But before he could respond, the uncertainty fled his nephew's features.

"We can go back to LA."

"No." His tone was sharper than he intended.

William crossed his arms and stared out the side window.

Zack softened his voice. "We're not going back to LA."

He'd love nothing more. If he could turn back the clock two months and five days, he'd do it. Back to before his sister's fatal accident. Before he'd given up his manager position and yet another promised promotion. Before he'd driven two thousand miles cross-country with an angry, rebellious teenager who seemed to think his uncle was at the root of all his problems.

Turning back time wasn't an option. All he could do was move forward. Keeping William in LA would have meant throwing away the boy's future. That fact had become clear when he'd stolen a four-wheeler with some friends and gotten arrested. So Zack had dragged him from the only place he'd ever known, away from his no-good friends who were putting him on a fast track to self-destruction. And he'd taken him to a tiny town he'd never seen before, based solely on the rave reviews of a high school friend who'd grown up here.

Somehow, he *would* get the kid straightened out. He'd never faced a challenge he couldn't conquer. He would come out on top this time, too. Except, over the past two months, he'd wondered more than once how he'd survive the next five years. There wouldn't be any help forthcoming from the boy's father. The man was in jail more than he was out. Currently, he was in.

Zack turned back to where the uniformed deputy was standing on the other side of the street, speaking into his radio. When he'd finished, Zack lowered his window.

"I live upstairs." Maybe he should have said *lived.* "Do you know if the lady who owns the jewelry store got out?"

"I don't think so. That's her vehicle there." He pointed toward a silver Jeep parked at the edge of the road that passed in front of the property. His face was creased with worry. He probably knew her. "I've called for help."

"I have my dog with me." He tilted his head toward the back seat. "He's trained in search and rescue. We'd like to help."

Relief flooded the deputy's features. "Yes, please."

Zack pulled off the road and exited his car. "Come, Ranger."

The black-and-tan coonhound jumped out and looked up at him. Excitement rippled through his body, as if he instinctively knew he was about to do something important. This wasn't their first search and rescue mission together. As volunteers with a couple of groups in California, they'd participated in several searches.

As usual, Ranger would work off leash. For the first time ever, he'd also be working without his vest. If it wasn't eventually recovered, or was too damaged, Zack would order him another one.

He leaned down to look at his nephew still inside. "You can get out and watch. Just stay at a safe distance and don't wander off."

William gave him a mock salute. "Yes, sir."

The words would have been encouraging if not for the sarcastic tone. As William exited the car, Zack glanced at the deputy's nameplate.

"Deputy Rutherford, I'm Zack Kimball, and this is Ranger. He has a vest, but it's somewhere in all that." He pointed at the wreckage. The deputy would have to trust him on Ranger's qualifications.

"Go ahead and have him do his thing."

"If he alerts, can we get some equipment in here to help uncover victims?"

"My brother owns a construction company over in Tiptonville and has a crane. He's on standby as we speak."

"Great."

Zack dropped to one knee in front of his dog, then slid his hands under his floppy ears to cup the brown face. "We've got a job to do. A nice lady's in trouble, and we need you to find her."

He straightened and held out an arm in front of him, index finger extended. "Seek."

Ranger looked up at him, a question in his big brown eyes. Zack had seen it before, the transformation that took place the instant the vest went on, the change from man's best friend to working dog.

"Yes, it's time to work. Seek!"

Ranger's hesitation lasted only a moment. He shot toward the wreckage and then gingerly made his way upward, boards shifting under his feet. Zack's pulse picked up speed. Working around collapsed buildings was dangerous. A dog could break a leg or sustain other injuries.

While Zack watched, Ranger continued making his way over the jumble of boards and other debris, face dipped downward except for when he'd lift his head to sniff the air. William stood on the sidewalk, watching the dog also. He was at a safe distance, and wandering off didn't seem to be crossing his mind.

Soon Ranger's movements grew more animated. He pawed at a board, sniffing with even more vigor. Then he released a sharp bark and sat.

"He found someone."

Cautious hope filled the deputy's eyes. "You're sure?"

"Positive." He'd been doing this with Ranger long enough to know. "We need to get your brother and his guys out here with that crane. I'd put an ambulance on standby, too."

"Absolutely." He placed the calls and pocketed the phone. "They're on their way."

Zack looked up at Ranger. He was sitting atop the debris, stock-still, waiting to be released.

"Ranger, come."

The dog descended as carefully as he'd gone up.

"Come here, boy." He dropped to both knees and cupped his face again, scratching him under the ears and working his way down the furry neck. "You did so good."

When he wrapped his arms around Ranger's middle, the dog turned his head to plant a slurpy kiss on Zack's cheek.

Zack laughed. "You're such a good boy."

He continued petting and praising the dog. Somewhere in the mess, alongside the vest, was a twisted rope with a ball attached to the end. After a search, whether or not Ranger was the one who'd found the missing person, Zack always rewarded him with a game of tug-of-war. Today's reward would be lots of love and praise.

Fifteen minutes later, an engine's deep rumble drifted to them. Soon it came into view—a huge truck with a crane mounted in its bed, lettering on the doors identifying it as belonging to Rutherford Contracting. Besides the driver, two other men were visible behind the windshield.

Zack put the dog in a down-stay as the man on the passenger's side exited the truck. Deputy Rutherford introduced him as David, his brother. Zack pointed out the place where Ranger had alerted.

"We're on it." He jogged back to where his employees waited. Soon the truck was in position and the men were hard at work, one operating the crane and David and his other employee on the ground assisting.

Zack watched the men remove rafters, beams and other debris from the pile, every muscle tense. One wrong move could cause the whole jumbled pile to shift and crush anyone trapped underneath. A quick glance at his nephew showed that he, too, was transfixed, unable to take his eyes off the scene unfolding in front of him.

The pile grew shorter as sections of wood and other materials were removed. Each pass with the crane opened a better path to the victim. As they worked, an ambulance arrived, and two paramedics exited and waited.

Finally, David bent over and called into the debris. From where Zack was standing, the rumble of the equipment drowned out the words.

After two more attempts, the deputy cupped his hands around his mouth. "Any response?"

"None. Whoever's down there might be unconscious."

Zack swallowed hard. At least the man didn't voice the other possibility.

Several minutes passed while the men worked, the rumble of the truck engine and whir of the crane making conversation difficult.

David straightened again. "I see a hand."

Zack released a pent-up breath. Soon they'd know her condition. If any customers had been in the store, he hoped everyone was in the same vicinity.

Now that some of the heavier items had been removed, David and the other man cleared boards away by hand.

David called out again. "Looks like it might be a man."

A man? What about Lauren?

The two paramedics retrieved a stretcher from the back of the ambulance, and David waved them forward. "Come on up. We've almost got him uncovered."

The paramedics made their way along the path that had been somewhat cleared for them. Then the four men worked together to finish extricating the victim.

David suddenly pivoted his face toward them. "Holy moly, he's wearing a ski mask." He looked back down and pushed another piece of debris aside. "There's a gun here."

Zack's jaw dropped. Was Lauren being held up when the earthquake happened?

Deputy Rutherford raised a hand. "Don't touch it."

He hurried to his vehicle and approached with a pair of latex gloves and a plastic bag. When he returned to his car a few minutes later, the bag held a pistol. Soon the paramedics had the man on the stretcher. The front and side of his shirt was dark with what looked like blood. They removed the mask and one checked for a pulse. A half minute later, he shook his head.

Zack looked at the deputy, heart pounding. "Lauren's still in there. I've got to get Ranger back up."

"Go ahead."

Zack again gave his dog the command to search. Ranger went back to work, and the paramedics made their way down with the stretcher. Instead of leaving, they put the deceased man in a body bag, radioed Dispatch for someone else to transport him and waited.

Ranger made a zigzag path, climbing higher. When a board shifted under his feet, he stumbled, then regained his footing. Several minutes passed with nothing. Maybe Lauren wasn't even there. Maybe she'd run out the back door.

No, someone would have seen her. She would have let people know she was safe. And she would have called for help for the would-be robber. No, she was still inside.

Finally, Ranger displayed the same excitement he'd shown earlier. His face was tilted downward, his nose inches from the debris beneath him, head moving side to side.

Rutherford drew in a sharp breath. "He found something, right? Isn't that what that means?"

Ranger barked and sat.

"That's exactly what that means."

Zack called his dog to him. After giving him lots of encouragement, he straightened to watch David and his men return to work. For the next hour, the action was a rerun of what they'd seen earlier. Shingles, roof decking and lumber came away, forming an ever-growing pile to the side. Some time ago, William had walked across the yard to sit with his back against a tree trunk.

David bent over, calling into the debris again. Judging from his demeanor, he didn't get a response. Zack looked behind him. The clouds that had dumped so much rain earlier were piled up on the western horizon. The sun was behind them. In two or three hours, it would be dark. If they couldn't get to her before then, would the men keep working?

He cast a glance at the deputy. Yes, they would keep working. Rutherford wouldn't let them quit until they found her.

David called again, then straightened suddenly.

"I got a response. It's weak, but I definitely heard 'help.'"

The deputy released a shout of celebration. Thirty minutes later, the paramedics were once again atop the collapsed building with their stretcher, pulling another victim from the wreckage. This one was alive. Silky blond hair flowed over the side of the stretcher. Rutherford released an audible sigh of relief.

The men's trek down wasn't smooth, and Lauren winced every time they jostled her. As they approached where he stood, her green eyes met his and she tried to smile. Small bits of debris were trapped in her hair, and several smudges marked her face, but she was still beautiful. "Sorry about your apartment."

He fell in beside them. "Sorry about your store."

"When I find my checkbook, I'll refund your rent and security deposit."

"Don't worry about that now."

She looked down at Ranger. "Did he help them find me?"

"He worked hard, but not as hard as those guys from Rutherford Contracting."

"I'm sure Danny was instrumental in getting them here."

Danny. Yeah, she and Rutherford knew each other.

The deputy had approached the other side of

the stretcher. "Was anyone else in the store with you?"

"Yeah. Right before the earthquake, a guy came in wearing a ski mask and carrying a gun. Rather than robbing me, he tried to abduct me." She closed her eyes, and a small shudder shook her shoulders. "Another man came in, also with a ski mask and gun. He wouldn't let the first guy take me, so the first guy shot him."

Rutherford pressed his lips together. "So, there were two men inside when the earthquake happened?"

Zack looked down at Ranger, ready to send him back up.

"No. The first guy took off. So only one was with me." She hesitated, her gaze no longer meeting the deputy's. "I hate to bring Lyle's name into this, but Jerry Beckham saw him last night, and he looked as if he'd been beat up. Then this guy comes into my store today and tries to abduct me. I don't know if the two events are connected, but I can't help feel they are."

She drew in a breath and winced. "Neither of the men who came in today was familiar. At least, I didn't recognize their voices. The second guy had a Spanish accent, a little different from Mexican. I'm not sure where he was from."

Rutherford's eyes met Zack's. They were probably thinking the same thing. The guy they pulled from the debris didn't look any more Hispanic than the two of them did. Lauren probably knew him, and he'd been trying to throw her off with a fake accent.

She rolled her head to the side to glance at the contractors who appeared to be awaiting further instructions. "Did they get him out yet?"

"Yeah."

"How is he?"

The deputy shook his head. "He didn't make it."

She pressed her lips together but didn't respond.

After a nod to his brother, indicating they were finished there, Rutherford put a hand on Lauren's shoulder. "I'll be up to see you when I finish my shift. Or I'll make it tomorrow if it's too late to-night. I have some more questions, but you need medical care."

"Can you have units drive by and make sure no one tries to take off with my merchandise?"

"How about if I get a hold of a security company and have a guard posted. Meanwhile, I'll stay here as long as I can."

"Thank you."

"I'm also getting a hold of hospital security, in case the first guy decides to try again." He looked at the paramedics. "Where are you taking her?"

"Pemiscot."

"Brian, guard her with your life."

The paramedic gave him a sharp nod. "Yes, sir."

Zack watched the men load her into the back of the ambulance. One climbed in with her while the other got behind the wheel. She'd likely receive any necessary emergency treatment on the way to the hospital.

Zack looked over at Rutherford, who was watching the ambulance leave. "Girlfriend?"

"Nah, man, more like a sister."

Zack nodded, an odd sense of relief sweeping through him. What was that about? It wasn't like any kind of romantic relationship would ever develop between him and his pretty landlord. Women avoided men with baggage. He had it in spades. His came in the form of a pint-sized kid with a boulder-sized attitude.

The deputy walked to his car and returned carrying a roll of yellow tape. "This won't keep out anyone who really wants to get in, but I'm hoping the message 'Police Line Do Not Cross' will be a deterrent, along with the units that'll be driving by."

When Zack and William got into the Mustang, the clock on the dash said five forty-two. Zack keyed "Pemiscot Hospital" into the GPS on his phone. It was only thirty minutes away, on the other side of the Mississippi River separating Tennessee from Missouri. He really wanted to check on Lauren. If they didn't keep her, she'd need a ride home. If she lived alone, he'd try to convince her to go somewhere else.

"What do you think of taking a trip to Missouri?"

"What's in Missouri?"

"The hospital."

William heaved sigh that said exactly what he thought of Zack's idea. "After I sat here all afternoon, you expect me to sit for several more hours at the hospital?"

"I'm sure there'll be a TV in the waiting room."

"With some dumb show that I don't even want to watch." The boy's eyes narrowed. "Get me a Nintendo Game Boy at Walmart, and I'll sit wherever you want for as long as you want."

William already had a video game console connected to Zack's computer, something Zack had tried to monitor since the kid had come to live with him. Of course, that console was toast, along with his computer.

"Deal." The poor kid had suffered yet another life-changing blow today. Giving him something to distract him was the least Zack could do.

"I want *Final Fantasy Adventure* and *Legend of Zelda* to go with it."

"If they're at Walmart, you'll have them."

"Walmart and dinner before the hospital."

"All right." Hospital security would see to Lauren's safety in the meantime.

"McDonald's."

"McDonald's it is." He shook his head. The kid

was going to be a lawyer someday. If Zack could keep him out of trouble long enough to graduate.

Walmart, McDonald's, then the hospital. By then, the doctors would have had time to run tests, and Lauren might have some answers about her condition.

In the meantime, her friend Rutherford would keep people from treasure hunting. The deputy had said she was like a sister to him. Good. At least Zack would be able to get to know his landlord better without ending up on the wrong side of local law enforcement.

Getting to know her better was exactly what he planned to do. He had no idea who this Lyle character was, but he'd apparently made some dangerous enemies.

And whatever his relationship with Lauren, she had somehow gotten sucked into a dangerous mess.

TWO

Lauren lay watching the clock, willing time to speed up. An hour and a half had passed since she'd arrived. It seemed more like four. At least she hadn't had to sit in the waiting room. Coming by ambulance, she'd been taken right to a bed in triage.

During the time she'd been there, they'd drawn blood, checked her vitals and done X-rays. The latter showed she didn't have any broken bones. But the doctor was concerned about the pain in the right side of her lower back and had ordered an MRI. She was still waiting for the results.

Even with a possible kidney injury, she'd fared much better than the man who'd come to her defense. Who was he? Why had he put his life at risk? Her stomach churned with the thought that he'd died while trying to save her.

Lauren shifted her weight, trying to relieve some of her stiffness. The ache intensified, the worst of it concentrated in the area of her right kidney. She hoped it was just bruised and would mend without treatment. Worst-case scenario, it was damaged beyond repair and would have to be surgically removed.

She pushed the thought aside. She was a best-case-scenario kind of girl, until there was reason to believe otherwise. At least her clothes were almost dry, although a little stiff. When they'd pulled her from the wreckage, she'd been cold, wet and miserable.

She shifted her gaze to the TV. It had been tuned to a news station since before she'd arrived. Everything that had aired in the past hour and a half had involved the earthquake, story after story of buildings damaged, homes collapsed, roads impassable, people picking through debris to salvage their belongings.

There'd already been two aftershocks, much lower in intensity than the main quake. Even that hadn't been severe, registering only 4.5 on the Richter scale. Today's event had been a gentle rumble compared to the quakes of the early 1800s. Those had flattened entire communities.

Outside the closed curtain, footsteps approached. Maybe the doctor had the results of her scan. Her chest tightened as she steeled herself for whatever news she was about to receive.

"Lauren?" The hesitant male voice didn't sound like the doctor's.

"Come in."

The curtain slid back on its track.

"Zack. What are you doing here?"

"Checking on you."

"Where is Ranger?"

"With William in the waiting room." He stepped closer. "You doing all right?"

"I'm bruised up, but nothing's broken, so that's a good thing. The table I was under collapsed, and its broken leg hit me in my kidney area. They did a scan to make sure everything's all right in there. I'm still waiting on the results."

He sank into the chair next to her bed. "What in the world happened?"

"What do you mean?"

"I left California for Tennessee, and a week later, my new digs are demolished by an earthquake. We expect them out there, but here? That's really messed up."

"We're in the New Madrid Seismic Zone. It's not as well-known as the San Andreas Fault, but minor earthquakes here are a regular occurrence. Usually we don't even feel them, but today was pretty bad."

"I won't argue with that." He paused. "Are you going home when they release you?"

"That's my plan. Maybe I can con my new tenant into giving me a ride to my car. It's still parked at the store."

"Absolutely. If you don't mind sharing a vehicle with a goofy dog and a teenager with an attitude." He grinned. "Although the attitude is much better since a trip to Walmart and a stroll through the gaming department."

"I take it he left happy and you left with your wallet a little lighter."

"You got it."

His smile widened. Her stomach did a flip and her pulse picked up speed. *Sheesh, get a grip.*

Maybe she was being too hard on herself. If her head was a little messed up, she had an excuse. She'd almost died today. Besides, Zack Kimball wasn't bad to look at. Those vibrant blue eyes, thick, dark hair and two-day stubble he sported made quite the combination.

The guy was raising his nephew, too. He hadn't told her how he'd ended up with the boy, but the fact that he'd taken on the responsibility said a lot.

Good looks and altruistic nature aside, he was her tenant. Until a few hours ago, anyway. Now he was homeless. With a kid and a dog.

Current or former, it didn't matter. The attraction she felt was inappropriate. She'd never had this problem before. Of course, her last tenants had been newlyweds five years behind her in school. She'd known them all her life. The one before that had been old enough to be her father. She'd known him all her life, too.

Actually, she knew him better than she knew her father, who'd taken off shortly after her mom's diagnosis, unable to endure the rounds of chemo and everything that went with it. Lauren had been seven at the time. Her mother had made it another ten years. When Lauren fought her own battle with the disease at age nineteen, her fiancé, Darren, had followed in her dad's footsteps. Through the years, contacts with her father had been limited to Christmas or birthday greetings…when he remembered. Contacts with Darren had been nil.

Zack grew serious. "Have you considered staying somewhere else?"

"Not unless my house is destroyed. Since it's brick, I'm hoping that's not the case. Why?"

He frowned. "Someone tried to abduct you from your store. What if the second man hadn't walked in? What if the earthquake hadn't happened?"

"I entered the panic code into the alarm panel. The police would have been en route."

"And by the time they arrived, you would have been stuffed in the trunk of a car, on your way to who knows where."

She closed her eyes, her chest tightening. What he'd said was true. She'd lost her store, but if not for the quake, she'd be…she didn't even want to contemplate the possibilities.

"Who is Lyle?"

Her eyes snapped open. Oh, yeah. She'd brought up Lyle's name before they'd taken her away in the ambulance. "My brother." He didn't need to know the details. Not that she was embarrassed. She'd long ago stopped feeling as if Lyle's actions somehow reflected on her.

"Speaking of Lyle, can I use your phone? I'm worried about him, and mine's buried." Along with her purse and camera and thousands of dollars' worth of jewelry.

A knot formed in her stomach. Her store, her merchandise, her brother's safety, the fear that he'd fallen back into a life of crime—she was an optimistic person, but everything was feeling like too much. She dreaded the coming weeks, dealing with insurance adjusters and everything involved in reconstructing her store.

Zack pulled his phone from his back pocket. "Here you go."

She tapped her brother's number into the keypad. With each ring, her uneasiness grew. Then his recorded message played.

"Lyle, it's me. Call me back at this number and let me know you're okay."

He had to be all right. Throughout most of their lives, they'd been at odds. They'd only been three years apart, but she'd been forced to take the parent role. Her mom had worked long hours to support them, and Lyle had needed a parent. When her mom had been bald and throwing up and too sick to get out of bed, Lyle had still needed a parent.

Her bringing him back to Ridgely had been good for them both. Over the past nine months, they'd become close for the first time in their lives.

Lauren ended the call and rested her hand in her lap, still clutching the phone.

Zack tilted his head, his eyes filled with sympathy. "I'm sure he's okay. During natural disasters, lines are often down."

"It's a cell phone."

"Okay, towers. They could be disabled or just jammed with so many people calling to check on friends and family."

"*Your* phone works."

"I might have different service. Give it time. If you want, when we leave here, I'll take you by his place and you can check on him personally."

"You would do that?"

"Absolutely."

"Thank you." Relief washed aside a little of the uneasiness. "Before I return your phone, can I make another call? I need to let my salesclerk know to not show up for work."

"Sure."

When Lauren told her about the condition of the store, Abby gasped. She hadn't heard. Lauren hoped she didn't rely too heavily on her paychecks. If she did, her parents would help her out. Since they all went to the same church, Lauren knew them well.

"Abby, I have a favor to ask. Kids Club tomorrow night, can you take my girls?"

"Absolutely."

"Maybe a few weeks after that, too?"

"Sure."

"Thanks." Not knowing what she'd be facing, having someone else handle that responsibility was a relief. It would also benefit Abby. She was taking classes at Dyersburg State Community College, with plans to major in elementary education.

After finishing the call, she handed the phone back to Zack. "Thank you."

Once again, footsteps approached and the curtain was pulled back even farther. The doctor stepped in. "How are you feeling, young lady?"

"Stiff, sore, but ready to go home."

"I think we can accommodate that." He looked at the electronic pad he held. "The MRI didn't show anything remarkable. Neither did your urinalysis and blood work. Creatinine, urea nitrogen, potassium, phosphorous, sodium—everything that might indicate acute trauma to the kidney, all within normal limits."

She released a breath she hadn't realized she'd been holding. *Thank You, Lord.*

He continued. "I'm sending you home, but I'm giving you a list of things to be on the lookout for. If you have increased pain, blood in the urine, swelling in the ankles and feet, nausea, vomiting, fever—anything out of the ordinary, get back in here."

"I will. Thank you."

"Good. A nurse will be in shortly with your discharge paperwork."

Twenty minutes later, Lauren walked into the waiting room, a small pack of instructions in one hand. Her other clutched Zack's arm. She'd said she didn't need a wheelchair. She would probably regret that decision by the time she made it to Zack's car.

William looked up from his game, the excitement of whatever he'd been playing fading from his face. Ranger rose and approached, tail wagging. The dog was happier to see them than the kid was.

Zack led her to the chair next to William. "I'm going to get the car." After commanding Ranger to stay, he looked at his nephew. "Keep an eye on her, okay?"

The boy nodded and returned to his game. He worked his thumbs in a rapid pattern. Something that resembled bursts of laser fire shot across the screen. Zack's instructions to keep an eye on her had obviously gone in one ear and out the other. As engrossed as he appeared to be, he wouldn't notice if a whole army of storm troopers walked in and dragged her out.

Not that she needed protection at the moment. Even if there was a legitimate threat, no one would be reckless enough to attack her in an emergency room lobby.

She looked down at the Game Boy. "What are you playing?"

He answered without looking up. "*Final Fantasy Adventure.*"

"That's the one where you're trying to keep the Dark Lord and his assistant from destroying the Tree of Mana and dooming the world, right?"

Now he did meet her eyes. "Yeah. You know how to play?"

"Not that one. I've just watched my brother play it a lot."

While he'd lived with her, he'd agreed to restrict his play to evenings. The first three months, he'd spent his days doing chores at home and odd jobs around town, as well as occasionally helping her in the store. Landing a full-time job had been a challenge. His prison record wasn't the only strike against him. He also had history to overcome. People had good memories. She'd finally convinced Steve at Precision Auto Repair to give him a break. *God, please let him be okay.*

William was still watching her. "What games *do* you play?"

"*World of Warcraft*, mostly." It had been ages since she'd played. She'd started as a teenager, hoping an activity with Lyle might keep him out of trouble. It hadn't worked.

"I play that with my friends sometimes. It's all right."

The automatic door slid open and Zack stepped

inside. She pushed herself up from the chair as he extended one arm. "Your chariot awaits."

"You're weird." The mumbled response came from behind her.

Zack rolled his eyes, and she accepted the arm he offered. Ranger trotted next to them, and William shuffled along behind.

After the boy and dog had climbed into the back, Zack helped her into the passenger seat. Finagling her legs inside kicked up her pain level several notches. An involuntary groan slipped past her lips.

Zack winced, the sympathy she'd seen earlier settling in his features. After sliding into the driver's seat, he pulled from the covered emergency room entrance. "Where does your brother live?"

"Midway Point. It's a small apartment complex in Ridgely, just six or eight units."

When he pulled into the parking lot thirty minutes later, Lauren leaned forward, her shoulders tensing. The building seemed to have sustained moderate damage. The long front porch was sagging and several windows were cracked. But the walls were still standing and the roof appeared to be intact.

"His car isn't here, but maybe someone brought him home."

When she reached for the door handle, he held up a hand. "You take it easy. I'll go up and ring the bell."

"He might not open the door for a stranger." Especially given what Jerry had told her about someone roughing him up.

Zack nodded, and she climbed from the car. After ringing the bell, she waited. All was quiet inside. She knocked hard on the door. "Lyle, it's me. Open up." Even as she shouted the words, she didn't expect an answer.

She trudged back to the Mustang and eased into the seat.

Zack was frowning at her. "Is it possible he's with a friend?"

"Maybe. I just have no idea who. His childhood friends are either in jail or are such bad influences that he's tried to stay away from them. He knows people from church, but at this point, they're more acquaintances than friends."

She pulled her lower lip between her teeth. "Can I use your phone again? Maybe he didn't hear it ring and hasn't noticed the missed call."

He handed her the phone. After four rings, his outgoing message began to play. She heaved a sigh and disconnected the call.

Zack again pocketed the phone. "What now?"

"I'll have to wait for him to call me back. If you can drop me off at the store, I'll drive myself home."

"Not alone. I'll follow you."

She opened her mouth to argue and snapped it shut again. She'd always been the strong one, the one to take care of everyone else. Tonight, she needed to lean on somebody for a change. Not only was there someone out there who intended her harm, she had no idea what she'd face at home. Losing her store was bad enough. How would she handle it if she pulled into her driveway to see remains of what had once been her house?

The trip from Lyle's apartment complex to her store took less than five minutes. Except for some cracked asphalt, the roads were in surprisingly good shape. The power was even on in most of the area. Zack eased to a stop behind her Jeep. Police tape wrapped the property, probably put there by Danny, but there weren't any law enforcement vehicles around. She hoped there'd be enough of a police presence to keep out looters.

She stepped from the Mustang, her stomach sinking. There was nothing left of her store or the apartment above it except haphazard piles of construction materials. She couldn't say whether anything had been disturbed since she'd been taken away. Her position flat on her back hadn't been ideal for surveilling her surroundings.

Zack's hand on her back drew her attention from the mess. "Are you ready to go?"

She nodded, a lump forming in her throat. The store had been her life for so long, even more so since becoming hers.

She squared her shoulders. Everything was covered by insurance. She would rebuild. It would take time, but eventually, everything in her life would return to normal.

A sheriff's vehicle drew to a stop behind Zack's Mustang. Danny Rutherford exited and approached. "I guess I won't be making that planned trip to the hospital. How are you feeling?"

"Stiff, sore, blessed to be alive."

"I still need to do a more thorough report, but I'll get with you in the morning after you've had a chance to rest."

She nodded. "I feel terrible for the man who didn't make it."

Danny's gaze dipped to the ground, and he shifted his weight to the other foot. They'd been friends long enough for her to read him.

A sense of dread settled inside, forming a cold knot in her stomach. Danny would have been there when the man was pulled out. His mask would have been removed, either by Danny himself or one of the paramedics.

She studied her law enforcement friend. "He was someone I knew, wasn't he?"

But that was impossible. Over the years, she'd had friends from Mexico and Guatemala, as well as a couple of the South American countries. The accent the gunman had spoken with hadn't matched any of those.

Danny stepped closer and rested a hand on

her shoulder. She tried to steel herself for the bad news she instinctively knew was coming— news that would shake the foundation under her more thoroughly than what this afternoon's earthquake had.

"Yes, you knew him." He swallowed hard, his Adam's apple bobbing with the action. "It was Lyle."

No. No, no, no. The denial circled through her mind, but the word lodged in her throat, never making it to her mouth. Her knees buckled, but she didn't hit the sidewalk. The next moment, she was clutched against a hard chest, Zack's powerful arms wrapped around her.

Lyle had been doing so well. He'd been working, going to church, staying out of trouble. She'd thought he had, anyway. She'd been wrong. He'd been conning her, just like he had so many other times through the years.

She'd fallen for it—hook, line and sinker. She'd opened her home to him, talked Steve into giving him a job, financed the old car he'd needed, and made the arrangements to secure the apartment. An overwhelming sense of betrayal settled deep inside, digging its talons into her heart.

Granted, he'd tried to save her. But he'd walked into her store carrying a gun, hiding his identity with the ski mask, the bulky rain slicker and that terrible Spanish accent. Did he owe someone money and had planned to rob her? What had he gotten involved in?

A hole opened up inside, the hollowness spreading throughout her core. It swallowed her shock, her anger, her grief, leaving her numb. At twenty-six years old, Lyle was gone. The last blood relative she had, except her father, and since she hadn't heard from him in over a decade, he didn't count.

Her brother was gone, but his bad choices were likely to outlive him.

How many of them would she be paying for in the coming weeks?

Lauren twisted in Zack's arms, and he loosened his hold on her. He wouldn't release her until he knew for sure she wasn't going to land on the sidewalk in a crumpled heap.

"Are you okay?"

When she turned to face him, tears glistened on her lower lashes, illuminated by the glow of the Mustang's headlights. She blinked them away. "I'm all right. At least, I will be."

"I'm so sorry. I know this has to be a huge blow for you." Not just his death, but the fact that he was in her store wearing a ski mask when it happened.

She nodded. "I'm ready to go home."

He hoped it was undamaged. Losing her store

and her brother in the same day had almost destroyed her. She couldn't lose her home, too.

Rutherford looked at him. "You'll go with her?"

"Absolutely." In fact, he wouldn't leave her until he knew for sure that she was all right.

Something about her made every protective instinct he had shoot straight into overdrive. Maybe it was her size—a good seven or eight inches shorter than his own six-foot height and probably not much more than half his weight. Maybe it was those expressive green eyes that seemed to reveal what she was feeling at any given moment. Or maybe it was the sweetness that exuded from her and wrapped everyone around her in its loving embrace.

Rutherford climbed back into his cruiser, and Zack walked Lauren toward the silver Jeep, still holding on to her arm. Halfway there, he hesitated.

"Wait. Aren't your keys buried in that?" He glanced at the demolished building.

"Yeah, but I have a spare hidden."

She walked to the back of the Jeep. When she started to bend over, he stopped her.

"Hold on." He pulled his phone from his pocket and switched on the flashlight app. "Tell me where it is, and I'll get it for you."

"Pop the hitch cover off."

Ah, inside the receiver. Not a bad idea. He

squatted and shone his light into the square tube. No key. He looked up at her over one shoulder, eyebrows raised.

"Lean down lower. You'll see it."

He did as instructed. Inside, a couple of inches deep, a piece of black duct tape lay almost flat against the top of the tube.

"Pretty smart."

"I can't take credit for it. I used to have it in one of those metallic boxes that attaches to the frame. Lyle said if someone wanted to steal my Jeep, that would be the first place they'd check. So he did this."

Zack peeled away the tape. The key was affixed to its back. Her brother had tried to protect her. He'd also apparently done something to put her in the sights of some very bad men.

He freed the key and handed it to her. "Is your house key hidden somewhere equally creative?"

"Not as well as this one. It's under one of the decorative stones in my front flower bed."

He rose, and a horn blew beside them. He turned in time to see William flop back into the rear seat of the Mustang.

Annoyance flared inside, but Lauren simply smiled.

"We'd better get going. I think you have a tired nephew. A tired dog, too."

"Maybe, but the dog is way more patient than the nephew."

"Have you ever known a teenager who has mastered patience?"

"You've got a point."

She climbed into the driver's seat of the Jeep, wincing with the effort. He waited while she cranked the engine.

"I'll be right behind you."

When he opened the Mustang's door, light flooded the inside. William hadn't moved from the back. Ranger lay next to him, his furry brown-and-black head resting in the boy's lap. His fingers moved in slow circles against the dog's cheek. In William's eyes, Zack had two things going for him—a cool car and a fun dog.

"Where are we sleeping tonight?" William asked.

"I don't know yet." The motels in the area were likely full.

"Can we stay with Lauren?"

He cranked the engine and watched the Jeep back from its space. "We can't just invite ourselves."

"Why not? She's hurt. She might need our help. Besides, you already paid her, so she sort of owes us a place to stay."

Zack shook his head. The kid definitely needed to consider a career in law. "If she invites us, we'll stay."

He really hoped she would. The three of them

sleeping in his car was a terrible option, but more importantly, he didn't want to leave her alone.

He eased out behind her, glancing in his rear-view mirror. A block or so back, headlights came on. Zack frowned. Maybe someone happened to be heading into town the same time they were.

Or maybe someone had been waiting, knowing she'd come back for her vehicle.

Zack followed her as she turned to head south on Tennessee 78. The vehicle behind him did the same. That didn't mean anything. The state route was the main north-south road through Ridgely.

As they headed into town, the vehicle behind them matched their speed. That wasn't cause for alarm, either. Lauren was traveling close to the posted speed limit. If someone was following them, though, Lauren would lead them right to her house.

William's eyes met his in the mirror. "What's going on?"

The kid was observant. "Someone might be following us."

William twisted to peer out the back window and then spun around again. "What are you gonna do?"

"Get Lauren's attention."

"How?"

"I don't know." When she'd agreed to rent to him, he'd saved her number in his contacts. With her phone buried in the wreckage, that wouldn't do him any good.

"Get up closer and blow the horn," William said.

"That might work."

He stepped on the gas and closed the gap until only two car lengths separated them. Instead of blowing the horn, he flashed his lights and signaled to turn right. Her brake lights came on and she negotiated a right turn onto Poplar Street. He heaved a sigh of relief. She'd picked up on his concern, even though she might not know why.

She continued west until reaching Main, where she turned right again. Zack frowned. She appeared to be driving with purpose, as if she knew exactly where she was going.

Oh, no. Was she still heading home?

Zack finished his turn and checked his mirrors again. Instead of following, the other vehicle made a sharp left and sped off in the opposite direction.

William twisted in the seat. "I think we lost him."

"He probably figured out we were on to him and gave up." For now, anyway.

When he followed Lauren through another right turn, a black Ridgely police cruiser sat under a double carport. By the time he stopped, Lauren had already parked and was standing at the open door of the cruiser, talking with the officer. The brick building beyond them housed the Ridgely Police Department.

As he approached, Lauren smiled at him. "I'm guessing we picked up a tail."

"Yep. Once he realized we were aware of him, he took off. The fact that you were heading in the direction of the police station probably helped, too. Smart thinking."

"I didn't know if I'd find anybody here but figured I'd give it a shot."

"It paid off." The officer smiled and extended a hand. "Officer Tamara Wilkins."

After he'd accepted the handshake and introduced himself, she turned her attention back to Lauren. "Your timing was perfect. I'd just stopped to finish a report."

Zack looked at Lauren. "So what now?" She was probably ready for the day to be over. He was running out of steam himself.

"Home. Can you make sure we're not followed?" She'd directed the question at the officer.

"No problem."

Lauren returned to her car, and soon, all three vehicles were headed south on Main Street, Lauren in the lead.

When she turned into a driveway several minutes later, the officer headed back toward town. Zack pulled up even with the Jeep and stepped from his car, eyeing the house in front of them.

It looked like a great starter home. It was made

of brick with a ten-or twelve-foot-wide porch breaking up the front. Curved beds wrapped the house on either side of the raised porch. In the glow of their headlights, blooming perennials stood out against a backdrop of shrubbery.

William and Ranger climbed from the car, and Lauren walked up to the bed on the left, stepping carefully between the plants. After tipping up a decorative rock, she rose, one hand raised.

"Ta-da. The key to the house. Since this is my only spare, I'd better get another one made. Although I'm rethinking my habit of hiding a key outside." She stepped onto the porch. "Come on in, all of you. First, we'll make sure nothing has collapsed. Preferably no broken windows, either."

Once inside, she flipped the switch by the door. Light flooded the living room. "We have power. That's a start."

William took a seat on the leather sofa. After telling Ranger to stay, Zack followed Lauren from one room to the next, checking ceilings for water stains and windows for cracks. Any possible damage to the foundation wasn't visible beneath the carpet, but there was no cracking in the floor tile in the kitchen or either bathroom.

They stopped in the living room where William was occupied with his Game Boy. "Everything looks good, but it wouldn't be a bad idea to have the place looked at by a real home inspector."

"I'll do that."

"I noticed an alarm panel when I came in. Is it monitored?"

"Yes. Ridgely is a pretty safe town, but having lived alone for most of the past ten years, I like the comfort of a security system."

"Good." That would make him feel better about leaving her alone.

"Where are you guys planning to stay?"

"I'm not sure. Any suggestions?"

"You'd probably have a hard time finding somewhere with vacancy. I have a guest room with a double bed." She gave him a sheepish smile. "After you saved my life, it would be pretty tacky for me to leave you to fend for yourself."

"It was Ranger that saved your life, not me."

Her smile turned teasing. "In that case, Ranger can stay and you guys can sleep in the car."

"Ranger was acting on my command, though."

"Okay, you win. I'd say I'll show you to your room, but you've probably figured out which one is yours."

"Yep, I used the process of elimination. If the makeup on the counter in the master bath hadn't given it away, the girly décor in the bedroom would have." He gave her a teasing wink.

"Hey, my décor isn't girly."

"The daylilies on the bedspread with matching curtains?"

"Okay, maybe a little."

Zack looked at William. "I'm taking Ranger out and bringing in our stuff. Then you need to brush your teeth and get ready for bed."

Besides the Game Boy, Zack had picked up some changes of clothes and toiletries for both of them. Tomorrow he'd see if any of their things were salvageable.

A few minutes later, he came back inside with Ranger and two Walmart bags. William took the one he handed him and headed to the hall bathroom without the usual bedtime battle. The kid must be exceptionally tired.

He was, too. Physically, anyway. Churning thoughts would hold off sleep for a while.

Lauren sank onto the couch. Fatigue showed in the lines of her face, but she was probably in the same place he was—too much on her mind to wind down and sleep.

He sat next to her. "Thanks for giving us a place to stay."

"You're welcome. But I'm still going to refund your rent and security deposit."

"Keep it. You're providing a roof over our heads, just not the one we planned on."

She gave him a half smile. "I'm glad you're here."

"So am I. But you really should think about making other arrangements."

"What other arrangements?"

"Somewhere else to stay, preferably far away from Ridgely."

"I can't leave. I've got too much to handle here—cleanup, a huge insurance claim, reconstruction. Final arrangements for Lyle. I can't do all that from another state."

She was right. Taking care of everything long-distance wouldn't be impossible, but it would be difficult. "You're not safe here."

"If the guy who tried to abduct me from the store is the one who was tailing us, he obviously doesn't know where I live. The fact that the driver waited who knows how long for me to return and then tried to follow me proves it. Otherwise, he would've been somewhere near my house, looking for an opportunity to carry out his plans."

"How long do you think it'll take him to find this place? Your car's sitting in the driveway. This isn't LA or New York City."

She pressed her lips together. "Okay, let's say I leave the state. Who's to say he won't find a way to follow me? When would it be safe to come back? I can't stay gone forever. My life is here. Whatever this guy's after, do you think he's going to just give up after a few weeks?"

She was right again. She wouldn't be safe until the man who'd tried to abduct her was behind bars. "You have no idea who he might be?"

"Not a clue. I'm sure I have Lyle to thank for the mess I'm in. I don't know if trouble followed him from Memphis, where he spent eight years before moving back here, or if he got involved with someone here."

She heaved a sigh. "Lyle's been in and out of trouble since he was thirteen, when he and his buddy hot-wired the neighbor's truck and went joyriding. They might have gotten away with it if they hadn't wrecked the truck on their way back into the neighborhood."

Zack winced. "Ouch."

"After turning eighteen, most of his offenses were minor drug charges. Then, three years ago, he really messed up." Another heavy sigh escaped. Her brother had obviously been the source of a lot of grief and disappointment. "He and a buddy got caught with thirty grams of meth. The only reason he's not still in prison is because he accepted a plea for a lighter sentence in exchange for testifying against his friend."

"How long has he been out?"

"Nine months."

"The other guy is still in?"

"Yeah. According to Lyle, he got a fifteen-year sentence. Lyle justified his ratting out his buddy by saying that he was the one who always lined everything up. Lyle claimed he didn't even know who they were working for."

Zack frowned. "If this is what's behind the threat against you, why did these guys wait nine months to act?"

"I don't know. Maybe they didn't know where he was. He's lived in Memphis since he turned eighteen. Even though this is where he was from, maybe it took them that long to catch up with him."

She looked down at her hands clasped in her lap. Silky blond strands fell forward, and she tucked them behind her ear. "I just can't believe I've been duped that badly. He seemed to be doing so well. Either he was conning me the whole time, or something happened that I know nothing about."

She lifted her head and turned to look at him. "I wonder if he was threatened with something if he didn't do what he was told. In fact, when he commanded the man who was holding me to let me go, the guy said that Lyle took orders from *them* and not the other way around."

"What do you think they had on him?"

"Me." She drew in a shaky breath. "Tracing him to Ridgely, they hit the jackpot. Not only did they discover where he'd gone, they learned he had a sister that he cared about. All they would have had to do to keep him in line was threaten to hurt me. In fact, Lyle told the guy that he was doing what he'd been told and was getting what he'd come for. Maybe he owed them money and holding me up was the quickest way to get it. He walked in carrying a gun and wearing a ski mask, so it would make sense."

Something wasn't adding up. "If Lyle was co-operating, why did the other guy try to abduct you?"

"I don't know. Maybe they were planning something else, something Lyle wouldn't want to be involved with. Holding me somewhere would be a surefire way to get him to do anything they asked." She paused, thinking. "If that's the case, I'm of no use to them anymore. Lyle won't care if something happens to me now."

"Why did they try to follow you home?"

"Maybe they don't know Lyle's dead."

"Maybe."

Then the threat would simply disappear. But he wouldn't stake her life on it. There were too many unknowns. In fact, everything they were coming up with was pure conjecture.

Her eyebrows drew together. "Right before the earthquake happened, the man who tried to abduct me saw something."

"What do you mean?"

"He looked past me at the counter, and his eyes widened."

"What did he see?"

"I don't know. It wasn't the jewelry displayed. He'd already told me he wasn't interested in that. It wouldn't have been the cash register, either, because he said he didn't want money."

"What else did you have on the counter?"

"Sales flyers, business cards, a framed ad for

an engagement set. I never found out what he saw. Right after that is when I set off the alarm, and then the earthquake happened."

She unclasped her hands to press them against the couch cushion on either side of her. "I'm wiped out." She pushed herself to her feet. "Is there anything I can get for you?"

"No, thanks. I'm going to call my parents. I've got to get to them before they hear about it on the news, or Mom will totally freak out." He smiled. "You know how parents are. I don't think they ever stop worrying about us."

She returned his smile, but it didn't reach her eyes. Maybe she didn't have the kind of parents he did.

As she headed down the hall, he moved into the kitchen and sat on one of the barstools. A half minute later, he had both parents on the line. They were shaken to learn what had happened but happy he had a place to stay. During the conversation, his mom asked him four different times if he and William were really okay. Losing one child had made her almost paranoid about losing the other.

When he'd finally convinced her they were safe, she shifted gears. "Have you come across any churches there?"

"Several."

"Maybe your landlord can recommend one. It would be good for William."

It probably would. Sara had started taking him about two weeks before her accident. He'd say her decision to attend church was one made of desperation, a last attempt to try to straighten out her rebellious son. But that wasn't the case. Someone she waitressed with had convinced her that a relationship with God would be the answer to all her problems. When she'd tried to push her newfound religion on him, Zack had politely declined. He didn't need a crutch. He'd always managed well on his own.

His parents had felt the same way…until Sara's death. When they suddenly found themselves floundering, without an anchor to hang on to, that was the first place they'd turned. Now his mom had taken up Sara's cause, trying to convince him that he had a hole in his heart that only God could fill.

"I'll ask her. She's lived here all her life." Even if she didn't attend, she would know people who did. He didn't feel any enthusiasm over the prospect of dragging William to church. The boy had given Sara lot of pushback. When Zack's parents had taken over that responsibility, picking him up from Zack's each Sunday morning, his attitude hadn't gotten any better.

"Speaking of your landlady, is she single?"

"She is."

"How old is she?"

"Maybe twenty-eight or thirty."

"You like her?"

"As a friend."

"You're not attracted to her." There was disappointment in her voice.

That statement couldn't be further from the truth. Lauren was beautiful. She was also sweet and compassionate and giving. "It doesn't matter."

His mother's dream of acquiring a daughter-in-law and eventual grandkids wouldn't happen anytime in the foreseeable future. For now, William needed his undivided attention. Zack didn't have anything left over to devote to a romantic relationship, no matter how special the lady in question was.

He finished with the call and carried the Walmart bag into the bathroom. Once ready for bed, he slipped quietly into the room across the hall. William lay unmoving, curled up on one side of the bed. Ranger lay stretched out on the other.

This wasn't going to work. One adult, a healthy teenager and a fairly large dog were too much for a full-size bed. As he gave the dog a shake and a hand signal to get down, a twinge of guilt passed through him. Ranger had worked hard today.

Zack shook it off. The beige-colored shag carpet was thick, and judging from the way it felt under his feet, it had a substantial pad beneath. Ranger would survive. Zack slid into the space vacated by his dog and pulled the sheet up with a contented sigh. The bed was comfortable, just the right firmness.

He closed his eyes, willing sleep to come. It didn't. He rolled onto his right side, his back to his nephew, but he couldn't get the beautiful woman in the next room out of his mind.

The thought of leaving her unprotected twisted his insides. But he didn't have a choice. He could probably take tomorrow off, maybe the next day, since his apartment had been destroyed. But if he expected to keep his new job, he'd need to get back to work on Friday.

Lauren had speculated that her assailant hadn't known Lyle was gone. The more Zack thought about it, the more unlikely it sounded. Her brother had been shot and buried under hundreds of pounds of construction materials. Even if the wound hadn't been immediately fatal, being left to bleed for several hours made the likelihood of survival minimal.

No, the man knew. But he'd still tried to follow her. Tonight, Zack had thwarted that attempt. But it was only a matter of time till he found her.

Zack would do everything he could to protect her. So would Deputy Rutherford. But neither of them could be with her twenty-four/seven. If the man was patient, he'd eventually find the opening he needed to make his move.

What if he struck when Zack wasn't there?

Not only would Lauren be in danger, William would, too.

Determination surged through him. He'd make sure that didn't happen.

Somehow he'd find a way to protect Lauren from whoever had put a target on her back.

THREE

Lauren waved at the workers pulling away in a dump truck and then took a plastic tote from William. Zack wasn't with her this afternoon. He'd had to leave shortly before two to report for his shift.

She'd hated to see him go. She wasn't sure what she'd have done without him the past two days. It was a new experience—leaning on someone else. She wouldn't get used to it, though. Having expectations of others only led to heartache. It was a lesson her father, and then Darren, had taught her well.

"Go ahead and get Ranger in the Jeep. I'll grab the last of the stuff."

Now that Rutherford and his guys were gone, she was anxious to get out of there. A sense of vulnerability had descended on her the moment the dump truck had disappeared from her sight.

William patted his side. "Come on, Ranger. Let's go."

The dog bounded toward him, long ears flopping. Zack hadn't wanted to saddle her with babysitting—his nephew or his dog—but he hadn't been comfortable leaving William home alone. So she'd offered to keep them both with her. It wasn't near the imposition Zack had feared. Just the opposite. On more than one occasion, she might have curled into a ball and cried had she been alone.

Two days had passed since the earthquake. Yesterday morning, Danny had come over to do his report. She'd recounted everything she could remember. Zack had sat on one side of her, the deputy on the other. She'd felt bolstered by both of them. She was going to get through this.

She'd also called Precision Auto Repair. Lyle had been there that morning and left at lunchtime, telling Steve he had some stuff to take care of and would be back around two. The words had hurt, knowing the "stuff" he'd referred to had likely included robbing her.

Had he willingly returned to a life of crime, deciding that was easier than making an honest living? Or had he simply gotten in over his head and hadn't known where to turn? If only he would have come to her.

Her final call yesterday morning had been to Dyersburg Funeral Home. Steve had told her the group life insurance policy he had through Precision would cover Lyle's final expenses. She planned to keep things as simple as she could, but having to make arrangements on top of everything else was about to push her over the edge.

Lauren slid the tote into the rear of her vehicle, which was backed up to the curb. The plastic box held several dozen file folders she'd retrieved from the four-drawer cabinet. Recovering them had required David's help, with the use of a Sawzall and a variety of pry bars. Her purse and computer were in there, too. The latter was badly dented. Whether it still worked would remain to be seen.

Yesterday afternoon, she'd met with the insurance adjuster and learned that her coverage included debris removal. Since then, David Rutherford and his men had hauled two loads of debris to the dump and filled two twenty-yard trash containers.

Zack had made good progress, too, salvaging what he could get to of his and William's possessions. The furniture hadn't fared well, but the books, photo albums and other keepsakes he'd had stored inside a chest had been unharmed. The majority of their clothing had been salvageable, too, requiring nothing more than laundering. Even Ranger's vest had come out presentable.

Lauren walked to what was left of the items she'd retrieved and slid one arm through the handle of a zippered bag. It held a kit containing a variety of pliers. Several of her tools had survived. Her camera bag was there, too, but the camera tucked inside was toast. So were all the lenses. The only reason she was keeping them was in case she needed to provide proof for the insurance claim.

She'd found her phone today, too. The screen was so badly cracked the phone was inoperable. Even without it, she hadn't felt isolated. Over the past two days, half the town had stopped to see how she was doing and offer condolences.

When she turned toward the Jeep, William was standing at the open passenger back door, trying to coax Ranger inside. From what she'd seen, the dog was usually obedient. Not today. Instead of hopping into the vehicle, he stood looking beyond her, posture stiff.

The uneasiness she'd felt expanded tenfold. She spun, but no one was there.

She hurried toward the Jeep with those final items. The sooner she could get them loaded and lock herself inside, the better she'd feel.

She'd almost reached the open back door when a low growl rumbled in Ranger's throat. He still stood outside the vehicle, his gaze fixed on a large oak tree about twenty feet away. Had he seen something? Was someone there watching her?

She stuffed the kit into the space next to the tote and tossed the camera bag in on top of it. As she stepped back to close the door, heavy foot-steps pounded behind her. She spun toward the sound, but before she could see who approached, a hard body slammed into hers, thrusting her against the rear door frame. The next moment, muscular arms wrapped her in a tight grip. Her feet left the ground. She released a scream, but a meaty hand over her mouth cut it short.

Ranger erupted in a flurry of barks and growls, charging toward them. Without putting her down, her captor kicked at the dog. Ranger leaped back to avoid the booted foot.

William was running in the opposite direction. Whether to seek out help or protect himself, it didn't matter. He was getting clear of danger. She only had herself to worry about.

The man holding her stepped back from the car. If he had plans to abduct her, she wouldn't go without a fight. Her arms were trapped against her sides, but she wasn't defenseless. She kicked at the man's shins and sank her teeth into the palm of his hand.

He jerked the injured hand away with an oath but still didn't release her. As he took another step, Ranger went airborne, his jaws clamping down on the hand she'd just bit. Her scream blended with the attacker's howl. Movement in her peripheral vision drew her attention. William was running toward them with a two-by-four.

The next moment, her assailant spun her in a

half circle and released her as Ranger let go. The ground rose at lightning speed.

She hit the sidewalk and rolled to the side, her body draped over the curb. Retreating footsteps grew softer. She pushed herself to a seated position. William stopped next to her and dropped his makeshift weapon, and she called Ranger over, as well. A short distance away, her assailant ran on to the next property. Her camera bag swung from his right hand. A moment later, he disappeared around the building.

Trying to pursue him wouldn't only be reckless, it would be pointless. He'd had too much of a head start. As if to confirm her thoughts, the roar of a vehicle engine came from that direction, and tires squealed. Moments later, there was a brief flash of blue before trees blocked her view of the fleeing vehicle. She flexed her wrists and rolled her shoulders, then twisted side to side. No new pains.

William looked down at her. "Are you okay?"

She pushed herself to her feet. "I think so." But what would she have done if Ranger hadn't been there?

"I was going to hit him with the board, but he'd already run away."

"I really appreciate it, but please don't do anything that could get you hurt." She paused, shaking her head. "He took my camera bag." He must have reached into her vehicle right after he'd thrown her to the ground.

William wrinkled his nose. "Why? That stuff's ruined."

"I know."

"Maybe he thought it was your purse."

That made sense. When he'd picked her up, she'd been afraid he was going to try to abduct her. Maybe he'd just been moving her out of the way so he could access what was inside the vehicle. "He's going to be disappointed when he finds out all he got was a smashed camera and some broken lenses."

She closed the back door. "I should report this, but by the time I borrow a phone, he'll be long gone."

"I think he's already long gone."

William was right. She would update Danny when she talked to him again, but she had so little for the police to go on. The vehicle was maybe a blue SUV. The man had dark hair cut close to his head and was a similar height and build to the man who'd attacked her in the store. Was that similarity a coincidence and this had been nothing more than a simple burglary? Or was there something much more dangerous behind today's attack?

"I need to get a phone." She'd already made that decision upon finding her old one today. She just wasn't looking forward to the drive to Dyersburg, a half hour south. Especially now.

"Can me and Ranger stay at the house?"

"I don't think Zack would be all right with me leaving you alone." Especially after this. But maybe he was safer home alone than with her.

He tilted his head down and lifted his eyebrows, as if she'd just made the dumbest statement ever. "What do you think he's been doing ever since he made me come live with him? I'm thirteen, you know. I don't need a babysitter."

She smiled. "I guess you don't. I'll drop y'all off at home."

While there, she unloaded what she'd recovered and pulled her damaged cell phone from the plastic tote. Maybe the Verizon salesperson would be able to transfer the data on her SIM card to her new phone.

Soon she was headed south on Tennessee 78, leaving Ridgely behind. Dyersburg was a straight shot. There wasn't even any traffic to speak of. Of course, the area was unpopulated, consisting of open fields and sparse woods.

She checked her rearview mirror for the sixth time since leaving the store site. So far, nothing had raised any alarms. But she wouldn't let down her guard.

When she arrived, the Verizon store was busy. She strolled the space while she waited, looking at the phone choices displayed around the perimeter. Thankfully, her property insurance would cover the cost.

"Can I help you?"

She turned from the specs she'd been reading toward the voice behind her. A young man stood there, about Lyle's age. His name plate identified him as Michael.

"Yes. I need a new phone." She pulled the damaged one from her purse.

He smiled. "What did you do, run over it?"

"It was a victim of the earthquake. The collapse of the building did it in. I fared better than my phone did."

His eyes widened. "You were in the building when it collapsed?"

"Yep. That's one experience I hope to never repeat."

His eyes widened even further, and his jaw went slack. "You're lucky to be alive."

"Not lucky, blessed." She'd never been one to take God's protection for granted. Even more so now.

"Do you know what kind of phone you're wanting to replace it with?"

She pointed to the one mounted beside the specs she'd just read. It was a Samsung, like her other one, just a later version. It wasn't the cheapest, but it wasn't anywhere near the top, either.

"Good choice. Let me get one from the back."

He disappeared and returned a few minutes

later with a small box. After leading her to one of the tables, he removed the phone from its packaging. "Let's see if the new phone will read that SIM card."

She handed him the damaged phone. As he removed the card and inserted it into the new phone, she held her breath.

"If your old one was still operational, we could transfer everything via the Smart Switch app. But if the SIM card isn't damaged, whatever's saved should transfer."

He put the cover back on the new phone, plugged it in and turned it on. After several taps, he handed it to her. When she pulled up her contacts, the list displayed. She released a relieved sigh. Her call log was there, too. She scrolled down, and the list ended. Same with her texts. "It only saved my most recent calls and texts."

"That's typical. SIM cards have limited memory. Everything else is saved in the phone's internal memory. If you've backed up to the cloud, you can retrieve data from there."

"I have, but it's been a while."

Like two years, maybe more. Danny's younger cousin had done it for her. Maybe he'd set it up to do recurring backups. That would be great... if she could figure out how to retrieve the information and get it to her new phone.

Maybe Zack could help her. If he couldn't figure it out, William probably could. Her generation was good with technology. The next was even better. They seemed to have been born with a technology gene.

After paying for her phone, she thanked Michael and left the store. As soon as she climbed into the Jeep, she keyed in a text to Zack.

Back in business. Leaving Verizon now.

She dropped her phone into her purse and pulled from the parking lot. It wasn't even seven o'clock. She'd be home well before seven thirty. When she and William finished eating, she'd see if he wanted to watch a movie. What kind of movies did kids like nowadays? If she expected him to sit through the whole thing, she should probably let him pick it out.

After she left the city limits of Dyersburg, traffic was sparse, with an oncoming car or truck whizzing past her sporadically and no vehicles overtaking her from behind. She made her way north, between fields stretching out on either side, broken by the occasional clump of trees. To her left, the sun sat perched on the western horizon, a fiery orange ball. Horizontal strokes of pink and lavender streaked the sky, begging to be photographed. She needed to get her camera replaced as soon as possible.

She slowed as she approached Bogota, the small farming community that lay between

Dyersburg and Ridgely. Behind her, a vehicle traveled too far back to be any more than dual headlights in her rearview mirror. As she drove through Bogota, those headlights drew closer. Shortly, that driver would have to slow, too.

Less than a minute later, she was through the small burg and past the halfway point on her way home. Although sunset was rapidly approaching, it wouldn't be fully dark for some time.

She stepped on the gas to bring her speed back up to the posted speed limit. Even though she was accelerating, the vehicle behind her was gaining on her. Uneasiness washed through her as she tightened her grip on the steering wheel. She forced the tension from her shoulders. She was overreacting. No one except William and Zack knew she'd gone to Dyersburg this afternoon.

Over the next couple of minutes, she cast frequent glances in her rearview mirror. The vehicle continued to close the distance between them. Any moment now, he would pull into the other lane. The road ahead was deserted. Nothing was keeping him behind her.

The distance continued to close. Ten car lengths. Nine...eight...

Come on, pass already.

Seven...six...five. The headlights were blinding, even in the dim light of dusk. Had he turned his brights on?

Four…three…

Maybe the driver had dozed off and was leaning hard on the gas pedal. She squinted to make out a figure behind the wheel. But all she could see was those bright headlights.

Two car lengths…one… She gripped the wheel and braced herself for impact.

The sickening sound of metal against metal reverberated through the Jeep. The impact slammed the back of her head against the headrest and sent the vehicle careening toward the opposite ditch. For the next several seconds, she fought for control, foot pressing gently on the brake as the Jeep took an erratic path down the highway. The right tires slipped off the roadway and the vehicle tilted before coming to a sudden stop in a drainage ditch.

Behind her, the vehicle that had struck her approached slowly. While she'd fought for control, he'd obviously held back. Had he struck her on purpose? Or had he simply dozed off?

Without knowing the answer, she wasn't about to face him alone on a deserted highway. She would make it to Ridgely and flag someone down, hopefully a police officer. Thankfully, neither the rear-end collision nor her hard stop in the ditch had deployed the airbags.

She pressed on the gas. The wheels spun. A quick glance in her rearview mirror ratcheted up her panic. The vehicle behind her had eased to the edge of the road about twenty feet back. She threw the gearshift into Reverse. Once again, the wheels spun. She was stuck. Behind her, the driver's door swung open.

She looked frantically around. There were no houses, only open fields. If she jumped from the Jeep and ran, whoever had hit her would be on her within seconds. There wasn't even anywhere to hide.

She retrieved her purse from the passenger floorboard where it had fallen and fished for her phone. When she straightened, a figure was framed in her side mirror, ten or twelve feet from her back bumper. He was short and stocky, just like the man who'd tried to abduct her. Just like the man who'd snatched her camera bag.

With shaking hands, she dialed 9-1-1. Her doors were locked. But the windows weren't unbreakable. Or bulletproof.

When the dispatcher answered, Lauren's panicked words flowed out in an incomprehensible jumble. Through the windshield, headlights moved toward her on the opposite side of the road, and she drew in a sharp breath. If she could get that vehicle to stop...

She flashed her lights, again and again, then had second thoughts. If the person who'd hit her meant her harm, she didn't need to put any innocent bystanders at risk. The dispatcher's voice came through the phone, asking what kind of service she needed. Lauren explained what had happened, coherently this time.

Through the front windshield, she watched the lights flash on the approaching vehicle as it slowed. Relief collided with fear. *God, help us!* She looked in her side mirror. The stocky man was probably right outside her door.

But he wasn't. He'd turned around and was already halfway back to his vehicle. Her breath escaped in a rush as she deflated against the seat.

The approaching vehicle stopped opposite her, just off the edge of the road, and the driver opened his door. A middle-aged man sat inside, dressed in overalls and a flannel shirt. She rolled down her window.

"Y'all need help?" Judging from the twang, he'd grown up on the eastern side of the state, or somewhere else in the Appalachian Mountains.

"The guy back there rear-ended me. I lost control, ended up in the ditch."

"The guy that just took off? I thought he stopped to help. I'll go after him, see if I can get a tag number."

She twisted in her seat. Sure enough, the person who'd struck her was driving like he was trying to outrun an avalanche. Red taillights were disappearing into the distance.

"No, he could be dangerous. I don't want you to get hurt."

"Don't you worry, little lady. I won't do anything risky."

As he pulled away, she turned her attention back to the dispatcher. "The guy that hit me took off. A Good Samaritan stopped and is going to try to get an ID on the vehicle."

"Okay. A sheriff's cruiser is about five minutes out."

Her phone buzzed with an incoming call. Zack's name came up on the screen. Why was he calling her from work? *Oh, no.* What if something had happened to William? She should never have left him alone.

"I've got a call I need to take. I'll be fine until the police arrive."

She switched over to the incoming call, heart racing. Zack wasn't going to be happy with her, and it had nothing to do with his nephew. He'd known she was going to Dyersburg tonight. He just wasn't expecting her to go alone.

But she couldn't demand a police escort everywhere she went. As far as William and Ranger, they were home, locked safely inside—exactly where they needed to be.

Zack didn't want her going anywhere on her own. But being with her was a danger to both his nephew and his dog. They needed to figure out who was targeting Lauren—and fast.

* * *

"Is everything all right?" Lauren's voice held an uncharacteristic tightness.

"Everything's fine. I'm on my evening break." He sat at the table in the break room, a heated frozen dinner in front of him. "I wanted to make sure you guys made it home okay."

A second or two passed before she answered. "William and Ranger are locked safely inside the house."

He frowned, a forkful of macaroni and cheese halfway to his mouth. What kind of a nonanswer was that? "You're not with them?"

This pause was even longer. "William wanted to stay home while I went to Dyersburg."

His chest tightened. His nephew was old enough to be by himself, and he wasn't likely to get into trouble at Lauren's house. That wasn't what bothered him.

"So you went alone?"

"Straight from home to the store and back, all in broad daylight. I figured it would be safe."

"Where are you? Why aren't you home yet?"

"I sort of had an accident."

He sprang up from the table, and his coworker turned from the microwave to look at him. Zack ignored him. "What kind of accident?"

"Someone rear-ended me on 78."

"Are the police with you?"

"They're on their way."

"So you're alone with the person who hit you?"

"No. When another vehicle stopped to help, he took off."

A hit-and-run, or an intentional attack that got foiled? Her story was going from bad to worse.

"Hold on." He left the breakroom in search of the shift supervisor. He found him still in the production area, clipboard in hand. "I have an emergency at home. I need to clock out."

Well, it wasn't *at* home, but it was related to home. He didn't have time to go into all the details. His supervisor gave the go-ahead, and he jogged toward his car.

"I'm headed your way."

"You've been on your job less than a week. Don't jeopardize it. The police will be here any minute."

He ignored her protests and headed back to the break room. That dinner he was looking forward to would go in the trash. As he picked it up from the table, another coworker walked in.

Zack held out the plastic container. "You want this? I haven't touched it."

"Sure."

He stepped from the room. "Where on 78 are you?"

"Maybe five miles south of Ridgely."

"The guy who stopped, you feel safe with him?"

"Totally. But he's not here. He went after the

guy who hit me to try to get a tag number and description of the vehicle."

"So you're alone?" Both his pitch and volume were higher than he intended.

"Not for long. I don't see the police yet, but I hear distant sirens."

A few miles outside of Ridgely, flashing red and blue lit up the road in front of him. He drew closer and pulled off opposite her Jeep. The only other vehicles were the sheriff's department cruisers.

He climbed from the car and strode to where Lauren was talking with one of the deputies, apparently describing the man who'd hit her.

"I was watching him approach in my side mirror. He wasn't tall, maybe five-seven or five-eight. He was stocky and had a buzz cut. It was getting dusk, so I didn't get a good look at his face, but I know it was roundish. Then the other guy stopped and he took off."

"Can you describe the vehicle that hit you?"

"Judging from the height of the headlights, I'd say a pickup truck or a larger SUV, maybe blue. He had his brights on. They would have been blinding if it had been fully dark. The other guy stopped, and I switched my focus to him. When I looked back again, all I could see was taillights in the distance."

A vehicle approached from the direction of Dyersburg. Its emergency flashers came on, and it slowed and pulled to the edge of the road. Lauren watched the driver's door swing open. "This might be my Good Samaritan."

A half minute later, a man in overalls was silhouetted in the headlight beams.

The deputy watched him approach. "You're our witness?"

"Not exactly. When I came on the scene, the young lady was already in the ditch. A blue SUV was pulled off some distance behind her. When I stopped, the driver made a U-turn and sped away. I tried to catch up with him."

Lauren stepped forward. "Did you get a tag number?"

"Nope. Just before Bogota, he turned onto Puckett Lane. Once the road straightened out, he floored it, made a couple of other turns and ended up headed south on Millsfield Highway. When he got up to eighty-five and was still accelerating, I didn't think it was worth it."

"Absolutely not. Thank you for trying."

The deputy moved closer. "Did you get a make or model?"

"Nope, couldn't get close enough."

The deputy clicked on his radio to put out a BOLO for a blue SUV. As he got the other driver's contact information, Zack followed Lauren to the damaged Jeep. Her insurance company was going to hate her, especially if the same carrier covered both her store and her vehicle.

She reached inside and straightened with her phone. "I'm obviously going to need a wrecker."

While she made the call, the man who'd stopped strode back to his truck, and the sheriff's deputy approached Zack. "I believe I'm finished here. Will you be with her till the wrecker arrives?"

"Absolutely." She wouldn't be able to run him off with a baseball bat.

The deputy returned to his car. As he drove away, his emergency lights went dark. Ten minutes later, flashing yellow lit up the road.

The truck stopped, and the driver got out. He and Lauren clearly knew each other. When he playfully gave her a hard time about driving into the ditch, she laughed. "I'm afraid I had some help. The vehicle that rear-ended me was a bit bigger than mine."

He hooked the cables to her Jeep and within a short time had pulled it from the ditch and loaded it onto the flatbed. When finished securing everything, he presented her with a form.

"Are you having us take it to our shop?"

"Yeah, I'm sure an insurance adjuster will be out within the next day or two to look at it." She signed the form and handed the pen and clipboard back to him. "Thanks."

"You need a ride home?"

"She can ride with me." Zack glanced at Lauren, and she nodded her agreement.

They watched the tow truck pull away, the silver Jeep chained to the flatbed. The whole back end was badly crumpled. He'd be surprised if the insurance company didn't total it.

He led Lauren to the Mustang and opened the passenger door. "Do you feel all right? You're not hurt or anything?"

"My neck might be a little stiff tomorrow, but I'm sure I'll get over it."

After closing her door, he circled around to the driver's side and slid in behind the wheel. When he cranked the engine, the dash lit up. According to the digital clock, it was after eight. "Have you had anything to eat?"

"Not yet. I'm guessing William hasn't, either. Or Ranger, for that matter."

"Maybe." Although William didn't always make the right choices, one thing the kid was good at was fending for himself. Sara had done her best, but with her work schedule, William had learned at a young age how to make sure he didn't go hungry, even if dinner involved no more than microwaved soup.

When they pulled into Lauren's driveway, the vertical blinds were turned at an angle, open just enough to see slices of the well-lit living room beyond.

Zack frowned. "That's something we should rethink."

"What?"

He killed the engine and opened his door. "Leaving the blinds open."

She pressed her lips together. "I've always felt safe here. I hate it that now I don't." She opened her door but didn't immediately get out. "Maybe getting hit today was an accident, like the driver fell asleep at the wheel."

"Then why did he run?"

"Maybe he was driving without a license and was afraid he'd be arrested."

"Do you really believe that?"

She expelled a heavy breath. "No."

He stepped from the car. By the time he got around to the passenger's side, she was already out and closing her door. He followed her into the living room, where William was watching TV. The boy wrinkled his nose at him.

"What are *you* doing home already? Did they fire you?"

"Thanks for the vote of confidence."

Lauren smiled. "He still has a job. Someone rear-ended me on my way home from the phone store, and my Jeep had to be towed. Your Uncle Zack brought me home."

William's eyes widened. "Man, some guy steals your camera and then your Jeep gets wrecked. Pretty stinky day."

Zack held up a hand. "Wait. What do you mean some guy stole her camera?"

He looked at Lauren. Was she seriously thinking of not telling him? How was he supposed to protect her if she wasn't going to be honest with him about the danger?

Why did he even feel the need to protect her? He wasn't law enforcement. Granted, she was his landlord. But that didn't obligate him.

There was just something about her. She was handling everything that had been thrown at her surprisingly well, but he sensed a lostness beneath the confident exterior. It kicked every protective instinct he had into overdrive.

Lauren sighed. "I was putting the last couple of items into the back of the Jeep. William was trying to get Ranger in, but the dog wasn't listening. He started growling, and then some guy ran up and grabbed me. When Ranger bit his hand, he threw me down and snatched my camera bag. He probably thought it was my purse." She laughed, but it sounded forced. "I'm sure he was ticked to find a smashed camera inside instead of a wallet full of money."

Zack frowned. Looting and other crime often followed a disaster. But there were too many other events leading up to this—the attempted kidnapping at the store, the tail they picked up on the way home, and now this. Who had Lyle gotten tangled up with this time? What could they possibly want with Lauren?

She continued across the room, walking toward the kitchen. "Did you guys have anything to eat?"

"I had a peanut butter and jelly sandwich and some Oreos."

Zack narrowed his eyes at his nephew. "How many Oreos?"

"I don't know. A few."

Likely more than could be counted on one hand. Maybe even two hands. The kid loved his sugar. Of course, what kid didn't? That was one of the jobs of the adults in their lives—to try to get something down them more nutritious than potato chips and Twinkies.

"What about Ranger?"

"I gave him some food out of the bag."

"Thank you." Zack followed Lauren into the kitchen, and the dog followed Zack. "I'll give Ranger his can of food. Then I'll give you a hand with dinner."

She smiled at him over one shoulder. "Thanks. I figured something easy—chicken Alfredo."

He saw to Ranger's meal quickly. As they moved about the kitchen preparing dinner, an unexpected sense of longing stirred inside him. This was what he'd always envisioned for his future—a beautiful woman at his side, working together with an easy camaraderie, a child or two in the next room. Lauren fit into that dream perfectly. He admired her and was comfortable with her.

He enjoyed spending time with her. He'd found her attractive right from the start.

Until recently, he hadn't been in a hurry to get serious with anyone. He'd had those milestones he'd needed to reach first—a healthy bank account, a great job, a nice home, maybe a boat. Things had been falling into place as planned. The promotion he'd been offered had been one of the last rungs in his climb, and he'd begun his search for a house, with a nice down payment sitting in his savings account. It was finally time to consider sharing his life with a special someone.

But that window of opportunity had slammed shut with his sister's accident. His responsibility now was to his nephew. William had his whole life ahead of him. Surely Zack could put his own on hold for another five or six years to try to keep William from throwing his away with bad choices. Lauren would understand, maybe even be willing to wait, but he wouldn't ask that of anyone.

Besides, his and William's stay here was temporary. Granted, they needed a home, but he could find somewhere to rent, if not in Ridgely, in one of the other nearby towns. No, his main reason for staying had nothing to do with the need for a home and everything to do with a beautiful lady who was in over her head.

She'd tried to convince him that the attack at the store site was nothing more than a purse snatching. She'd even suggested that the accident was a simple hit-and-run. But no matter how many explanations she offered, he wasn't buying them. She obviously wasn't, either. What had her brother done to endanger not only his own life but hers also?

Try as she might, she couldn't deny it. Someone intended her harm. Maybe that someone even wanted her dead.

FOUR

"Can we play *World of Warcraft?*"

Lauren looked at William, sitting in the passenger's seat of her rental Jeep. When Zack had gotten home last night, she'd expressed her concerns about William's safety. They'd finally decided he'd be safer with her than staying home alone. So he and Ranger had been with her all afternoon.

As always, William held the ever-present Game Boy. Instead of playing, he was looking at her, waiting for an answer to his question. She'd started off the day meeting with a representative of Dyersburg Funeral Home to make final arrangements. Instead of a formal funeral, she planned to have a memorial service at their church once things settled down. She'd brought in the obituary she'd written, along with a photo that was so Lyle—the blond hair that was always a bit shaggy, green eyes that held a hint of laughter and a crooked smile that made him look as if he was up to some sort of mischief. Looking at it had made her heart ache even more.

As emotionally draining as the meeting had been, she'd headed straight to the store site afterwards. What she wanted to do now was go home, microwave leftovers and veg in front of the TV.

"Sure, we can play."

As she approached Family Dollar, an old pickup backed from one of the parking spaces. She passed and watched in her rearview mirror as it moved toward the exit and pulled onto Main Street.

The truck closed the gap between them until the bearded face of the driver was visible through the windshield. But she knew that truck and the owner. The beat-up Chevy was one of a kind, a good two decades older than she was.

William looked in the side mirror. "Is that truck following us?"

"Yep."

His eyes widened.

"It's okay. It's just Ralph."

"Who's Ralph?"

"A farmer who lives about a half mile from me."

The boy visibly relaxed. "So he's okay."

"Totally harmless."

"He has animals?"

"Just chickens. But he grows a lot of crops. When things settle down, I'll take you guys to meet him. He'll send us home with lots of fruits and veggies."

"Corn on the cob?"

"Maybe, but we're at the end of the season for that. Do you like watermelon?"

His eyes lit up. "Yeah."

"Apples and pears?"

"Yeah."

She squelched a smile. "Broccoli?"

He crinkled his nose, and she laughed.

"I'm guessing Brussels sprouts are out, too."

"Eeewww, gross."

"While you're with me, I promise I won't make you eat any broccoli or Brussels sprouts…unless they're smothered in cheese."

He didn't agree, but he didn't argue, either. The same comment from his uncle would have triggered some vocal resistance. Over the past three days, the attitude Zack had mentioned had come out several times, but none of it had been directed at her. Of course, she wasn't the one responsible for making sure he grew up into a decent, productive human being.

William twisted and reached between the bucket seats. "Hey, Ranger."

As he turned back around, he dragged a small plastic tote into his lap. "Can I look at this stuff?"

"Sure."

She'd salvaged a good bit of her jewelry. It had

been a painstaking process, picking through the shattered glass and other debris.

After removing the lid, William slid his fingers through the items inside and held up a tennis bracelet with a variety of colored precious and semiprecious stones.

"This stuff's pretty. It looks expensive. Where do you get it?"

"From jewelry wholesalers. I make some of it, too."

"You do?" The raised eyebrows indicated he was impressed.

Tonight, once she had everything notated on her inventory spreadsheet, she'd lock it up in her small safe at home. When she'd salvaged everything from the store site, she'd take it all to the bank and rent some safe-deposit boxes.

"What level are you?"

"Level?"

"Your character."

Oh. He'd already lost interest in the jewelry and was thinking about the game.

"It's been so long since I played, I'll probably have to create new ones."

"If you have your password, you can still get to them."

"Maybe." She'd just have to remember log-in credentials from almost ten years ago. She didn't even use the same email anymore.

As she headed out of town, she checked her

mirrors again. Ralph was still behind her. No one was behind him. When she turned into her driveway, he sped past, tooting the horn in greeting.

She killed the engine. "You want to help me carry this stuff in?"

"Okay."

She climbed from the Jeep, stifling a groan. She was still sore. Getting knocked to the ground yesterday hadn't helped. Over the past three days, her body had been turning interesting shades of black and blue and yellow. It would take time for the bruising to disappear. The pain in her right kidney was just a dull ache. None of the symptoms the doctor had warned her about had shown up.

Danny Rutherford had been keeping her updated on the investigation, which so far had yielded nothing. Everyone in the homes and businesses near her store had been hunkered down inside during the heavy rain and hadn't seen anything. Although authorities had looked, there'd been no sign of a blue pickup or SUV with a smashed front end. She'd updated Danny on yesterday's attack in front of the store, but nothing had come of that, either.

William followed her to the house with two of the totes stacked on one another. She led him into the combo kitchen/dining room, carrying two others, which she put on the table. He placed his next to hers.

"One more trip should do it."

Soon they had everything inside. Other than jewelry, there wasn't much. Furniture was broken or water damaged. Office supplies weren't salvageable. The laptop she'd brought home yesterday hadn't survived. She'd checked it out this morning and hadn't been able to get it to boot up.

Her personal laptop sat at one end of the table, waiting for her to make her entries. Since she kept her records in cloud storage and always logged every piece, it would be obvious if anything was missing.

Her old laptop was sitting on the living room coffee table. When William had noticed it on the closet shelf, he'd been quick to point out that since she had two computers, they could game together. That was all right. Her hours gaming with Lyle hadn't accomplished anything, but maybe building that connection with William would.

An hour after finishing their dinner of reheated chicken Alfredo, they'd completed a simple quest. She closed her laptop.

"Time to hit the sack."

"Can't we do another one? It's only nine o'clock."

"I'd love to, but I've got to get all of that cataloged." She waved a hand toward the table behind her, where the four totes waited. "We'll play again soon. I promise."

William sighed, but the sound seemed to be more disappointment than grumbling. "Okay."

When he left the kitchen, she logged into her cloud storage and opened her inventory list. For each item found, she would note its condition—undamaged, repairable or insurance claim.

She'd just gotten started when the water came on in the bathroom. Apparently, William was brushing his teeth without having to be told. She'd report that, as well as the fact that he'd gone to bed without argument, to his uncle.

Sometime later, she laid the last piece of jewelry on the sizable stack in the safe and closed the door. The clock on her bedside stand said ten thirty. No way was she going to make it till Zack got home at eleven fifteen. He'd have to use the duplicate key she'd given him yesterday.

She took Ranger out the kitchen door, into the fenced back yard. The five-foot-high vinyl panels had been installed by the prior owner to keep deer and other critters out of his garden. Though she'd never had time to garden herself, she appreciated the privacy, especially now. Somehow, taking Ranger into the fenced area felt much safer than walking him around the fully exposed front yard.

The dog immediately lifted his leg on her shrubbery and hurried back inside.

"Thanks for making that quick."

In the hall, she opened the spare bedroom door

just enough for him to disappear inside. The glow of the living room light fell across William's face. In sleep, all traces of adolescent bravado had fled. In fact, he looked vulnerable, even a little bit lost.

Just like Lyle had during his unguarded moments. She'd failed Lyle. *God, please let me make a difference in William's life.*

The dog hopped onto the bed and stretched out next to the boy, leaving no room for a full-grown man to join them. Zack would have to figure out sleeping arrangements when he got home. She closed the door and turned off the lights in the front of the house, leaving the porch light on. Zack could arm the alarm system when he came in.

Fifteen minutes later, she crawled into bed. She was just slipping into sleep when scratching brought her instantly awake. A whimper followed.

Seriously? Ranger couldn't have to go again already.

She rose and had almost reached the spare bedroom when a sound at the front door halted her steps. Was Zack home already? He wasn't due for another twenty minutes.

She moved in that direction, planning to let him in once she'd checked the peephole. After taking one step into the darkened living room, she stopped. The glow of the porch light wasn't coming through the opaque side glass. Had the bulb burned out?

Or had someone unscrewed it?

Now there was a series of scrapes that sounded more like a tool against the frame than a key being inserted into the lock. A shadow moved in front of the narrow side window, briefly blocking the dim glow of a nearby streetlight.

She spun and dashed down the hall at a full run. Her phone was in her room, charging on the nightstand. She snatched it from its charger and hurried toward the other bedroom, touching the phone icon and tapping the three numbers. No way would help arrive in time, but trying to reach the back door wasn't an option. They'd likely meet the intruder in the living room.

Several sharp barks punctuated the silence of the house. Ranger didn't have to go. He'd heard the would-be intruder and had been trying to warn them. As soon as Lauren opened the spare bedroom door, the dog bolted from the room as if he'd been shot from a cannon, sideswiping her left leg. She stumbled backward, and her phone slipped from her hand.

Moments later, a flurry of barks came from the living room, interspersed with deep growls. She retrieved her phone and sent through the call she'd started.

William emerged from the room. His curly

dark hair was flat on one side and sticking out in loose spirals on the other. "What's going on?"

She gave him a soft push toward the open door. "Someone's trying to break in. Go back in the bedroom and lock the door."

The boy's eyes got huge. "What are you gonna do?"

"I'm—" She hesitated. She'd planned for all three of them to wait inside the locked spare bedroom.

What would Zack do? Would he leave his dog to face an intruder alone or try to coax him into the room? Except right now, the dog was too riled up to be coaxed anywhere.

The dispatcher's voice cut across her thoughts. She backed into the room with William and locked the door. "Please send police. Someone's trying to break into my house."

The dispatcher confirmed the address and promised that help was on the way. Instead of ending the call, she encouraged Lauren to remain on the phone. Lauren swallowed hard, willing the police to get there quickly. When she looked at William, he stood with his back pressed against the wall, eyes wide with fear.

Lauren stepped closer to pull him against her side. He didn't resist. She lowered her voice to a whisper. "Police are on their way. We'll be okay."

Suddenly, Ranger fell silent. He was probably recharging for his next round. Or maybe the would-be intruder had decided he'd rather not fight with a dog.

Then the creak of the front door hinges sent her heart into her throat. A single bark followed. Then silence. *Dear God, help us.*

"They're inside. The front door just opened." Even at a whisper, her voice held a hysterical edge. "I think they hurt Ranger."

"Hold on." The dispatcher's tone was soothing. After a short pause, she continued. "The police are less than five minutes away. Are you in a safe place?"

"We're locked in the spare bedroom."

"Stay put."

Lauren looked frantically around the room. There was nothing she could use to protect them. There wasn't even a good place to hide. The room was sparsely furnished, containing just the bed, the dresser and a desk.

She released William and pointed toward the floor. "Get under the bed." Even with her storage totes, there'd be space for him. She'd be hard-pressed to fit under there herself. Although William was close to her height, his slender frame hadn't yet begun to fill out. "Stay there until I say it's safe."

Once William had scrambled under the bed, she slid the closet door silently back on its track. The space was almost empty. The bulky winter clothes she stored there occupied only one-third of the rod.

She scanned the items on the shelf. There was a bowl she tossed coins into, a box of candles, extra toilet paper and paper towels, a stack of blankets and a small space heater.

Nothing she could use as a weapon. Unless…

After passing the phone off to William, she lifted the space heater from the shelf. It wasn't heavy, but it had fairly sharp corners. If she swung it down hard on someone's head, it could do some damage.

She moved into position next to the locked door, elbows bent, heater held against her chest. She'd wait for the intruder to kick in the bedroom door. Before he could react, she'd attack. Maybe by then, the police would be entering.

It was a terrible plan. But it was the only one she could come up with.

God, please let this work.

Zack set the alarm and bent over to cup his dog's face. As soon as he'd opened his car door, he'd heard ferocious barks coming from inside the house. His heart had shot straight into his throat…until he'd found the place dark and locked up tight. Lauren and William had obviously gone to bed, and Ranger was taking his new position as guard dog seriously.

He gave the dog a couple of pats on the head.

"Let's go to bed. And be quiet so we don't wake up the others."

The dog followed reluctantly, casting frequent glances back at the door.

"What's up with you?" Had he heard a noise? Something must have gotten him riled up. One thing was sure. No way would an intruder get into the house as long as Ranger was there.

A siren sounded in the distance, barely audible. He stepped into the hall and tried to quietly turn the bedroom doorknob. It didn't budge. He gripped it more tightly and twisted harder, then tried the other direction.

Great. What was William ticked off about now, enough to lock him out of their room? He hadn't spent enough time with the kid today to get on his wrong side. Of course, if he had a *right* side, Zack hadn't seen it during the past two months.

He heaved a sigh. He needed to give the boy the benefit of the doubt. Maybe he felt safer with the door locked. With everything that had happened the past few days, he had every reason to be scared.

He raised a fist to rap lightly, then hesitated. The door at the end of the hall was open. The last thing he wanted to do was disturb Lauren's much-needed rest.

His other option would be to sleep on the couch. He'd have to wear his work clothes since his gym shorts were in the bedroom.

Actually, there might be a third option. He turned on the bathroom light and looked at the bedroom doorknob. It was an interior lock with a small, circular hole in the center. If he had a paper clip, he could get in. Or a small screwdriver, like the one on the mini multitool he carried.

As he pulled the item from his pocket, the siren reached its peak volume and suddenly died. Whatever had occurred was obviously close. A sense of uneasiness settled over him. Were the vehicles responding to whatever had had Ranger so upset?

He needed to check on Lauren. After just one step, he stopped. No, he wouldn't charge into her room while she was sleeping. If William was all right, she was, too. Besides, based on what he'd heard tonight, if anyone had wanted to harm Lauren or William, they'd have had to take down his dog.

After finding the right tool, he inserted it into the hole. A metallic click told him the lock had released. A fraction of a second later, heavy banging on the front door reverberated through the house. Ranger went crazy, dashing toward the front. Ferocious barks mingled with shouts from outside.

Zack swung the bedroom door open. Lauren stood in the shadows, an object held over her head.

Shouted words came from the front. "Lake County Sheriff. Come out with your hands up."

Zack flipped the switch, and light flooded the room. Lauren stood staring up at him with horror-filled eyes. "What are you doing here?"

"You invited me to stay."

"You're early."

He opened his mouth to respond as William's head appeared from under the bed and another command came from the front. Whatever was going on, law enforcement didn't need to be kicking her door off its hinges. He hurried to the living room, disarmed the alarm and swung open the door.

Two men in uniform stood on Lauren's porch, two more on the ground, standing one on each side of the three steps. All four had pistols aimed at him.

As he raised both hands, Lauren appeared next to him.

"Bruce, James. He's okay. He's not the intruder. He arrived after." She stepped back. "Come on in."

Both men had lowered their pistols. So had the two standing at the bottom of the stairs. One of them called up to the others.

"We'll check the area. Let us know as soon as you get some intel on who we're looking for."

When the deputies had stepped inside, Lauren closed the door and showed them to the love seat—Bruce and James, although he had no idea which was which. Lauren seemed to be on a first-name basis with everybody.

Zack eased onto the couch, and Lauren sat next to him. After William situated himself at the other end, Ranger lay on the floor and rested his furry head on the boy's feet.

One of the deputies removed a notepad from his shirt pocket. Worton, according to his name-plate. He was apparently going to be the lead investigator. "You called saying someone was trying to break into your house. Any idea who it might have been?"

"No. All I could see was a shadow in the side-light. I think he was working with a tool, trying to get in."

Zack followed the other deputy to the door where they both studied the frame. The wood held pry marks, likely made by a screwdriver or chisel as the intruder had tried to pry the dead bolt free.

"I'll dust this area for prints." He radioed the two who'd remained outside and instructed them to be on the lookout for anyone in the area who looked suspicious, even though they had no description. Then he walked away to retrieve his fingerprint kit.

When Zack walked back toward Lauren, she was smiling at his dog. "The intruder would have gotten in if Ranger hadn't heard him and started scratching at the bedroom door. When I let him out, he charged into the living room ready to tear up anyone who came through that door."

Pride swelled in Zack's chest, along with love for his dog. The friendly black-and-tan coonhound had come to him through the National Training Center in Santa Paula, California. Trained in search and rescue, he wasn't a guard dog. But he was protective of his people. Zack was the alpha male, but William had become part of Ranger's pack. It was obvious the dog was quickly accepting Lauren into his pack, too.

After a series of questions, Deputy Worton asked Lauren if she had anything else to add.

"I'm not sure. Like I said, I don't know who it was that tried to break in. It might have been random, someone thinking that, with only one car in the drive, there might be a woman alone inside. But it's possible I was targeted, too."

She filled them in on everything that had happened since the masked man had walked into her store the day of the quake. "I can't tell you anything about whoever tried to break in tonight, but the guy who tried to abduct me, the one who snatched my camera bag and the one who rear-ended me are all short and stocky. My guess is we're talking about the same person."

Worton nodded. "We'll try to get some units driving by here on a regular basis."

"Thanks, Bruce. Zack is here, too, when he's not working. He and William were renting the apartment over my store, so they're here for the time being."

"I'm glad you're not alone." He frowned. "I've been worried about you since Lyle came back, not knowing what you might get dragged into."

"You and Jerry Beckham and half the other people in this town." She shifted her attention to Zack. "I'm guessing you didn't see anything when you pulled in, or you wouldn't have seemed so clueless when you snuck into the spare bedroom."

He shook his head. "Ranger must have scared them away before I got here. I was sneaking in quietly because everything was dark. I didn't want to wake you guys up. When I saw you hadn't even turned on the porch light for me, I figured you were exhausted."

"I did turn it on. I thought maybe the bulb had burned out." She stepped outside, and when she started to reach into the fixture, the deputy stopped her. With a couple of twists of his gloved hand, the light came on.

"I'll try to lift some prints from the bulb, too."

When he'd finished, Worton rose and handed Lauren a card. "Call me if you think of anything else."

She closed the door behind the deputies, and Zack ruffled William's hair. "Okay, sport, the excitement's over. Time to go back to bed."

William looked as if he would protest but, after a glance at Lauren, he rose with a sigh. "Come on, Ranger. Let's go to bed."

Lauren watched him disappear into the hall, the dog following, and then sank onto the love seat. When Zack sat next to her, she shook her head. "I almost hit you. If the police hadn't called out when they did, I would have brained you with the space heater."

"And I wouldn't have blamed you." He was impressed. Lauren obviously wasn't going to go out without a fight. "It didn't help that I'd gotten home early. We finished one order and with only ten minutes left in the shift, it wasn't worth starting the next, so they let us go. In the future, I'll text you to say I'm on my way." He smiled, then grew serious. "Speaking of the future, what are you going to do?"

"I don't know."

"We've had this conversation before. Now I feel even more strongly. You're not safe here."

She pulled her lower lip between her teeth and stared at the opposite wall. "I know. Let me think about it."

"Do you have family, aunts and uncles?"

"Neither of my parents had siblings, so no aunts, uncles or cousins."

"Your mom?"

"She died when I was seventeen."

"I'm sorry. Your dad?"

"He took off shortly after my mom was diagnosed. I haven't heard from him in more than a decade."

His chest tightened. Was she really that alone? When he'd lost Sara, he and his parents had grieved together. At her funeral, he'd been surrounded by aunts and uncles and cousins and friends. It was such a stark contrast to what Lauren was describing. Could he somehow help fill that void?

Lauren continued. "Most of my friends are in this area. I have a few that have moved away, but I've lost contact with them over the years." She met his gaze. "It sounds like I have no life, but I really do. It's a fairly full life. It's just all right here."

She pushed herself to her feet. "I'll think about what you said. But tonight, I'm too tired. Tomorrow's another long day. I'm meeting David Rutherford at seven again, so I've got to be out of here in a little over six hours. He's hoping to get most of the rest of the debris cleaned up."

She checked the door and armed the alarm system. "If you're awake when I leave, I'll see you in the morning."

"We'll be up and ready to go when you are." William would have a fit, but no way would he let Lauren venture out alone, especially after tonight's events.

He followed her into the hall and slipped into his own room while she continued to hers. As quietly as he could, he exchanged his work clothes for some comfy gym shorts.

Now that his eyes had adjusted, the room wasn't totally dark. Moonlight and some of the porch light's glow seeped in around the blinds. Neither of the two lumps on the bed moved. Both boy and dog appeared to be fast asleep. Zack would try to not disturb his nephew. His dog was another story.

He dropped his voice to a whisper. "Come on, boy. Down."

Ranger stretched and yawned and then relaxed again without changing positions. The dog was exceptionally obedient. Most of the time.

Zack pulled him toward the edge of the bed. "Come on, Ranger."

He wrapped his arms around the dog's middle and shifted seventy-five pounds of limpness from the bed to the floor. Then he stretched out on the comfortable mattress, fingers intertwined over his abdomen.

The tension slowly seeped from his muscles. He was tired. His body was, anyway. His mind, not so much. As worried as he was about Lauren, there was William to think about, too. Leaving him here put him in the same danger she was in.

But moving somewhere that he'd be left unattended for forty or fifty hours a week put him in a different kind of danger. Every community, even small ones, had its seedy side. William was the type of kid who had a knack for finding trouble.

Living in the apartment, he'd had a little peace

of mind knowing Lauren was downstairs until six in the evening. He'd asked her upon moving in to text him if she noticed anything of concern. He'd also gotten a landline installed in the apartment. It had served a dual purpose—William could call for help in case of an emergency, and Zack could check in during his evening break. If the kid had hoped to sneak out and get into trouble, he would have had to do it between the time of that phone call and when Zack arrived home after his shift.

The situation was different now. Until school resumed, William had too much free time on his hands. Spending that time with Lauren was the best thing for him.

Letting his thoughts circle back to his pretty former landlord didn't do anything to help bring on sleep. Deputy Rutherford had promised to have units regularly drive by her store until she retrieved all of her merchandise. Tonight, Deputy Worton had said he'd try to get the same security for her home. Parking a unit right outside would be even better.

He hoped he'd convinced her tonight to leave Ridgely. She'd said she'd think about it. Handling everything from another state wouldn't be easy.

But it would be impossible if she was dead.

FIVE

Lauren watched two dump trucks pull away, tarps stretched over their heaping loads. That wasn't the last of it. The rusted boiler that had provided heat for the building back in the day, though unused for decades, had never been removed and lay crushed among the remaining floor joists, plumbing pipes and electrical conduit. Other debris still lay scattered about, but her property no longer looked like a bomb had gone off.

Zack stepped up beside her. He'd been with her all day. Since it was Saturday, he hadn't had to report for work.

"You're getting there."

"Slowly but surely."

They were both pretty confident they'd retrieved everything from the wreckage that was salvageable. All that remained was a little bit of cleanup, which David had promised to complete Monday morning.

"So what'll be next?"

"Rutherford Contracting will put together a construction bid. Once the insurance company makes the first installment, they'll pull the necessary permits and begin the work."

"Any idea of a time frame from start to completion?"

He was probably curious about when he and William might get back into their apartment.

"Optimistic, five months, but we're probably looking at closer to six or seven."

He and William were welcome to stay as long as they wanted, but they were probably anxious to have their own space. Knowing Zack, he wouldn't even consider a move until the danger to her was over. That protectiveness endeared him to her even further. Between the sacrifices he was making for his nephew, his care and concern for her, and those irresistible good looks, hanging on to her heart wasn't easy. But she would somehow do exactly that.

He was attracted to her. She'd seen it in his eyes. But he didn't know her history, what lay dormant in her body. If he knew, he would bail, just like her father had. Just like Darren had. Cancer wasn't easy to deal with. Knowing it would likely strike again without warning was even harder. In her experience, men didn't deal well with that kind of uncertainty. Maybe Zack was different, but she wasn't willing to risk her heart to find out.

Zack called to William, who'd alternated between sitting under an oak tree with his Game Boy and getting up to play fetch with Ranger. In the middle of the day, while she'd continued working with David Rutherford and his men, William and Zack had driven into Tiptonville, fifteen minutes north of them, to pick up sandwiches from Subway. When they'd gotten back, they'd worked with the Google Drive login information she'd provided and downloaded everything that was missing on her new phone. Thankfully, Danny's cousin had set her old one to back up everything automatically.

William sprang to his feet and ran to them, Ranger beside him. The kid hadn't complained, but he had to be getting bored. "Are we going home?"

"Not yet."

William heaved a sigh, and Zack turned to Lauren. "We want to take you out to dinner as a thank you for letting us stay with you."

The boy instantly perked up, but Lauren frowned at Zack.

"You already paid for your accommodations. When I tried to give you your money back, you refused. So, no thanks are necessary, and you certainly don't need to buy me dinner."

Zack planted both hands on his hips. "Are you really going to deprive us of an enjoyable evening out with our pretty former landlord?"

"The enjoyable evening out is fine, but I'll pay my own way." She ignored the *pretty former landlord* comment, as well as the unwanted flutter that his descriptor created in her stomach. *We're just friends.* If her brain repeated those words enough, maybe her heart would start to listen.

He shrugged. "Okay, you win."

Lauren looked at him with narrowed eyes. He'd agreed too readily.

Zack led her toward the Mustang. "I'll drive. I want to check out the Grecian Steakhouse in Dyersburg."

When he pulled into the restaurant parking lot thirty minutes later, he nabbed one of the last spaces. As expected, the place was busy. With its reasonable prices and great buffet, it was a popular place to eat.

He stepped from the car and flipped his seat forward for William. The boy climbed out and cast a glance back at the dog. "Can Ranger come in?"

"Once I put his vest on." He looked at Lauren. "I'm not sure what your laws are in Tennessee, but I never leave him in the car."

She wasn't sure, either. In some states, it was illegal. "He's a good boy. I don't think he'll be trying to raid the buffet."

Zack laughed. "Nope. But I'll order him some grilled chicken unseasoned."

It took them thirty minutes to be seated. Since they all ordered the buffet, they didn't have to wait for their meals. The server promised to bring Ranger's portion when it was ready.

Once Zack had put the dog in a down-stay under the table, Lauren got into the buffet line, ready to load her plate with salad. Zack was right behind her. William headed straight for the dessert.

Zack dropped out of line to follow. "Hey, no dessert until you've eaten some real food."

"Chocolate cake *is* real food."

"Okay, food that doesn't have enough sugar in it to make a polar bear hyperactive."

"I'm old enough to make my own decisions."

"I'll believe that when you start making wise ones."

William's gaze met hers briefly before bouncing back to his uncle. No way was she stepping into this. The kid was testing his boundaries. His uncle had to be the one to set them. And enforce them.

William moved away from the dessert to plop a piece of chicken and some fries on his plate. Apparently, that was good enough for Zack. The kid wasn't going to fill his plate with salad.

When they got back to the table, William dug into his fries with gusto, and Lauren briefly bowed her head to offer thanks for the food. By the time she'd made it halfway through her salad,

William's plate was empty. She wasn't surprised to see him walk to the dessert bar and spoon up a sample of everything on it. If he was a kid who got wired with sugar, he was going to be up all night.

Zack watched him briefly and then shifted his attention to her. "Since Rutherford's guys won't be back until Monday, what's on the agenda for tomorrow?"

"Church."

"I was hoping you'd say that."

"Really?" She couldn't help the smile that spread across her face.

"I wanted to get William plugged in somewhere."

She raised her brows. "Just William?"

He gave her a half smile. "It might do me some good, too. I've never been big on religion, but lately, I've been rethinking that."

"Because of William?"

"Along with some other things."

He didn't expound on what those other things were. William returned to the table, his plate heaping with sugary treats. Zack finished his salad just ahead of her and then followed her to the buffet. When they returned, William leaned back in his chair with a satisfied sigh, the plate in front of him empty. His gaze followed the server who was walking toward them with Ranger's grilled chicken.

"Can I feed Ranger?"

"Sure."

He picked up the plate and disappeared under the table. When he stood and started to walk away, Zack frowned. "Okay, buddy, that's enough sugar for one sitting."

"I'm not getting more dessert."

"Where are you going?"

"To the bathroom, if you don't mind."

Maybe Zack didn't mind, but William's tone said *he* certainly did. Zack was right. In his nephew's eyes, he really couldn't do anything right.

She watched the boy disappear into an alcove at the other end of the restaurant. "How did you end up taking care of William?"

"My sister—his mom—was killed in a car accident two and a half months ago."

His words were a punch to her gut. "I'm so sorry. That has to be awful for both of you."

"It's been tough."

"Is his dad in the picture?"

"Occasionally, when he's out of prison, which isn't the case right now. His brief reentrances into William's life have centered around his need for a bed and a hot meal rather than any sense of responsibility toward his son."

"When he gets out, do you think he'll try to get William back?" She hoped not. The boy needed consistency, something Zack was offering.

"I doubt it. If he did, I can't conceive any court

offering him custody. Besides his history, he and my sister never married, and he never claimed legal responsibility for William."

"Good. Right here with you is the best place for him."

"Not in William's eyes. He doesn't think I do anything right. Everything's a battle, and it just keeps getting worse. He hates me for taking him out of LA. I don't really blame him. He loses his mother, and then two months later, I tear him away from his school, his friends, and everything he knows. I did it for his own good, but he'll never see that."

He shook his head. "I'd always planned to have children someday, but I never expected to have a mini man dropped in my lap. I'm so out of my element."

His confession felt like a kick in the gut—not that he was struggling, but that he wanted children of his own.

Of course he did. A lot of single men shared that sentiment. If not now, they often did once they settled down and matured. She knew better than to expect any different. She and Zack were friends, and that was all they would ever be. She'd be content with that. Friends shared. And friends offered comfort when comfort was needed.

She gave him a sympathetic smile. "He'll eventually see that your bringing him here was the best thing that could have happened to him."

"I hope so. It wasn't a spur-of-the-moment decision. For the last six months, he'd been getting into trouble. Sara was doing her best, but even with the help I'd offered, she'd always worked two jobs to keep food on the table and a roof over their heads. William's had too much time without adult supervision."

He drew in a deep breath and released it in a sigh. "Back in California, he snuck out while I was sleeping and met up with some friends. They broke into a shed and were making off with a four-wheeler when the owner woke up. The boys all scattered, but William got caught."

"Oh, no. What happened?"

"The owner was a guy I'd gone to school with. He wanted to give William a second chance and agreed to drop the charges. I knew then that if I hoped to keep the kid from following in his father's footsteps, I had to get him out of there." He shrugged. "So here we are."

She covered his hand with one of hers. "You're doing a good job with him. You can't see it now, but it'll pay off."

He turned his hand over to give hers a squeeze, his gaze warm. It was filled with appreciation, but something else, too. Yeah, he was attracted to her. The pull on both sides was strong. She could so easily fall for him. If only...

Across the restaurant, William emerged from the restroom and made his way toward them.

Lauren moved her hand, and Zack dropped his voice even further, speaking rapidly.

"I hope you're right. He *has* been doing better since the earthquake. I have you to thank for that. He seems to like you."

"I like him, too. He's a good kid deep down." A good but hurting kid. One she wanted to wrap in her loving arms and vanquish all his pain. She just wasn't sure how to do it.

"Maybe he is. You have a knack for bringing that out."

"He probably thinks I'm cool because I played *WoW* with him."

William reached their table and looked at Zack with narrowed eyes. "Were you talking about me?"

"Sort of. Lauren was saying you guys played *WoW* last night."

William looked at her for confirmation.

"Yep, I was."

His gaze shifted between them several times before he sat. When they'd finished, their server laid the checks on the table. Zack snatched Lauren's before she could react.

"I told you I was paying for mine."

"I got to it first, so you're out of luck. You can return the favor when you've got your store back up and running."

"My policy covers loss of income." It wouldn't

be what she normally netted, but it would be enough to pay her bills.

"How soon do you think it'll be before you get your first check? Conserve what you have. I've got this." He reached into his pocket for his wallet.

Soon, obligations were handled. Lauren walked with him from the restaurant, William in the lead holding Ranger's leash.

When they reached Ridgely, Zack circled back by the store so she could pick up her rental. A few minutes later, she turned into her driveway and Zack pulled in next to her.

She was the first one inside. Upon entering, she disarmed the alarm and flipped the light switch. She was halfway through the living room when a soft thump came from the back of the house.

She froze, heart pounding out an erratic rhythm. No, no one could be inside. The alarm had still been armed when she entered. She dropped her purse on the coffee table and moved into the kitchen. As her gaze snagged on the bar, a bolt of panic shot through her. The two computers she and William had used were now stacked on one another, the damaged one lying on top. The cords were rolled up next to them.

She spun and ran into the living room as heavy footsteps pounded down the hall. The next moment, she came face-to-face with her intruder. Her heart leaped into her throat, and a shriek escaped before she could stop it. She had to get out of the house and warn Zack and William.

Just as she reached the front door, an arm wrapped around her waist and pulled her back. Her assailant reached past her and twisted the deadbolt with a latex-covered hand. Now she was locked inside with him.

He dragged her toward the kitchen. *God help me!* He was going to take her out the back. Behind her, there was the barely audible sound of the deadbolt sliding over slowly. The man holding her tensed. He released her suddenly, scooped up the laptops and ran for the back door.

The next moment, the front one swung open and Ranger charged through the living room toward them, Zack and William behind him. The back door swung shut.

Zack stopped in front of her, panic still swimming in his eyes. His gaze swept the length of her and then snapped back up to her face.

"I'm all right," she said. "He was inside. He took the laptops, ran out the back."

Zack closed the distance to the back door in two swift steps and swung it open.

"No!" She grabbed his arm. "You're not armed. He probably is."

It was too late to stop Ranger. He was already in the back yard, sharp, rapid barks piercing the night. Lauren followed Zack out in time to see the man lift himself over the fence. Ranger's jaws clamped shut on thin air where the man's foot had been a fraction of a second earlier. After a few more barks, the dog turned and trotted back toward the house.

Zack had his phone out and was already dialing 9-1-1. The man's head disappeared below the top of the fence and then reappeared before he took off running. He'd probably dropped the laptops over before climbing over himself.

Once Zack had the dispatcher on the phone, he briefly relayed what had happened and handed the phone to Lauren to give a description of the man.

They stepped back inside. Once she was finished, she disconnected the call. "They're going to send someone."

Zack pocketed his phone and walked into the living room, where William was sitting on the floor petting Ranger. "I'm sorry we didn't come in right away. We were waiting for the dog to do his business. Was the security system armed when you came in?"

"It was. So how did the intruder get in without setting it off? All the doors and windows have sensors."

Without responding, Zack began to walk around, opening blinds and looking at windows. When he reentered the dining room and walked to the other side of the table, glass crunched under his feet. He lifted the blinds. Most of the glass in the lower sash was gone.

He inspected the window. "These are open/close sensors. I'm guessing you don't have any glass break sensors."

"Apparently not. I've had the system for a long time. You can be sure I'll remedy that first thing Monday morning. At least I'll get the ball rolling."

While waiting for law enforcement to arrive, she and Zack walked through the house, checking each room. Other than closet doors being open, nothing was disturbed.

They'd just walked back into the living room when the doorbell rang. The deputies standing on her porch were the same two who'd been in her home last night. She'd gone to school with Bruce. James was a friend's older brother.

She invited them inside and offered them a seat on the couch. "We went out to dinner and I walked in to find an intruder in the house."

She relayed everything to them, up through finding the broken window.

"Can you describe the intruder?"

"About five-seven or so, stocky, not obese as much as solid, like a football player. His face is roundish, clean-shaven, medium complexion. He has dark hair, really short, a buzz cut. I can't say for sure about the masked man who came into my store the day of the earthquake or the one who attacked me outside, but I'm pretty sure the face I saw in my living room tonight was the same one that was framed in my rearview mirror yesterday."

Bruce looked up from the notes he was taking. "Is anything missing other than the laptops?"

"We checked, and nothing appears to be disturbed," she said. "When he ran out the door, he wasn't carrying anything except the laptops. Maybe he'd planned to take more and got interrupted when we came home."

Bruce nodded. "If you notice anything else, let us know. You've still got my card from last night?"

"Yes. I need a copy of the police report, too, so I can file a claim with my insurance company."

When she returned to the kitchen, William was sitting at the bar, elbows on its surface and chin resting in his hands. He looked up at his uncle. "Me and Lauren won't be able to play *WoW* anymore."

She pulled out the other barstool and sat next to him. "We will eventually. I have insurance to cover them."

Zack leaned against the end of the bar. "Do you find it odd that someone would break in and steal laptops while leaving everything else untouched?"

"Like I told Bruce, we interrupted a burglary in progress."

"Two days ago, your camera was snatched."

His eyes were narrowed, his lips pursed. "What if the men are after pictures you took?"

"Why? I photograph animals and scenery, sometimes people. I've won a few photography contests, but nothing I've done has any value." She gasped as realization slammed into her. "The man who tried to abduct me. I told you he saw something. He wasn't looking at the counter. He was looking beyond it, to the table against the back wall. My camera was sitting there next to my computer, a cable connecting them. I'd been at the park right before this and had taken a bunch of pictures. I'd just finished uploading them to the cloud."

She shook her head. "He probably would have snatched both the camera and computer then, except right after that is when I hit the panic code on the alarm and the earthquake happened."

She rose and started to pace. "We need to view those pictures as soon as possible. I'll call my friend Kat and ask to borrow her computer." After a quick glance at the clock, she frowned. "It's late. I'll talk to her after church tomorrow."

"Good, because I'm guessing at least one of those photos holds the answers to our questions."

The strains of the final song faded to silence. Like the other worshippers, Zack eased into the chair behind him. The little white church sat on the outskirts of town and looked like it wouldn't hold more than a hundred fifty people fully packed. Today it was close to capacity.

He and Lauren sat halfway back on the left side of the sanctuary. When they'd first walked in, two teenagers who'd entered ahead of them introduced themselves to William and invited him to sit with them.

Zack's first inclination had been to say no. Without adult supervision, his nephew would be shooting spit wads or finding some other way to disrupt the service. Before he'd had a chance to respond, William had accepted the invitation and followed the two into the center aisle.

Lauren had assured him that William would do fine, that the boys were the preacher's son and nephew and were good kids. As he and Lauren had started up the aisle, the three boys had marched all the way forward to join a group of other teens seated in the two front rows.

He'd decided then that Lauren might be right. If those kids were bad news, they'd be huddled together in the back rather than sitting under the watchful eyes of everyone in the congregation.

The pastor stepped to the pulpit and introduced the scripture that would be the basis for that morning's sermon. It was the first chapter of Habakkuk. He couldn't say he'd ever heard a sermon preached on the Book of Habakkuk, not that he'd sat under that many sermons.

Zack's gaze shifted to his nephew's head of

curly dark hair. As he'd stood four or five rows behind him during the praise and worship time, he hadn't been able to tell whether William was singing. Now he couldn't say he was listening to the pastor, either, but his face was turned in that general direction and he was sitting still. In Zack's eyes, that was a win, considering that, before even leaving the house, they'd had a major blow-up over Zack telling him he couldn't bring his Game Boy.

The scripture appeared on the two screens on either side of the platform. Given all the uplifting stories in the Bible, the pastor had chosen a pretty depressing passage. When Habakkuk had complained that God wasn't listening to his cries for help, God had told him that he was sending the Babylonians to exact judgment. What an answer. No wonder Habakkuk had responded with another complaint.

By the time the message was over, Zack understood the point the pastor was making. He encouraged his congregation to get real with God, to express their doubts and fears and questions, that burying those things led to resentment.

Zack couldn't say he resented God, but if given the opportunity, he'd love to ask some questions of his own, such as why had God taken Sara and left William essentially orphaned? Why had this responsibility landed in his lap when he'd had everything so well under control? And why had he been stuck with two choices that were equally unacceptable—giving up everything or sacrificing his nephew's future?

When the service ended, Lauren introduced him to those who'd been seated around them. He stole a glance up the aisle, where he expected to see William making a beeline for him, ready to ask when they could leave.

Instead, the kid was still at the front, standing with a group of four or five teenagers, including the two who'd introduced themselves before the start of the service.

Zack returned his attention to Lauren, who had her hand on a woman's shoulder. "This is Kat. We've been best friends since second grade."

When she'd finished with introductions, she dropped her hand from her friend's shoulder. "I have a favor to ask."

"Anything for you, girlfriend." Kat's smile was broad, her eyes dancing with enthusiasm. With that friendly smile and the energy she exuded, she possessed a cuteness that pulled people in.

"I need to use your computer."

"What's wrong with yours?"

"I had a break-in last night. Coming home from dinner, I actually walked in on the guy while Zack and William were still outside with Ranger. He ran out the back with my laptops."

Kat's eyes grew huge. "Oh, no. I'm so glad you weren't hurt. Of course, you can use my computer."

While Lauren and Kat chatted, Zack searched out his nephew again. The boy was finally making his way toward him. Instead of his usual bored shuffle, his face held a sense of excitement.

William stepped into the row and stopped next to him. "The youth group is having a pizza party and then going bowling. Can I go?"

Wow. For most of the boy's life, he'd sought out the troublemakers. Now he was wanting to actually hang with some church kids? "Sure. How much money do you need?"

Indecision flashed across William's features as he looked at the others still gathered at the front. Finally, he met Zack's gaze again. "They said I don't need any. They have enough money in the youth fund."

Zack stifled a smile. During those moments of hesitation, the kid was probably trying to decide whether to attempt conning money he didn't need.

Bringing William to church had been a smart choice. Maybe one or two of the friendships begun today would continue. These kids didn't seem likely to be smoking dope or breaking into houses.

Maybe William wasn't the only one who needed to be here. All his life, Zack had believed he had everything under control. But that control had wavered with his sister's crash, and every day he spent with William, another piece of it slipped away. With the realization that he wasn't in charge of his own life came something else—an odd emptiness, a void. Maybe it was the hole in his heart that his mom had referred to, something she insisted that only God could fill.

While the pastor had talked about Habakkuk's questions, he'd thought of several of his own. But what about the deeper questions, ones he'd never pondered before? Questions like *Why am I here? What is my purpose? Is this life really all there is?*

When he and Lauren climbed back into the Mustang, it held one fewer occupant than when they'd arrived. The youth minister had assured them that he'd take responsibility for William and return him to Lauren's house when they were finished bowling.

She fastened her seat belt and looked over at him. "Kat invited us for lunch. I accepted for both of us. I hope that's okay."

"Sure."

He had no friends here, so he was happy to hang out with Lauren's, especially if it meant deepening his friendship with her. In another life, he would have been interested in more. Lauren was beautiful, inside and out. Everyone clearly loved her. What was not to love? She was caring, compassionate, sweet and smart. He was surprised she was still single.

She liked him. Maybe she was even attracted

to him. But anything beyond friendship was out of the question. For the past decade, he'd devoted his life to moving up the ladder at the metal processing plant where he'd worked. Now, his priorities had shifted. Instead of working sixty- and seventy-hour weeks to attain the future he had planned, he'd vowed to spend that extra time building a bond with his angry, rebellious nephew. In doing so, he might be able to steer him away from choices bound to ruin his life. It wouldn't be easy, but it might be the most important thing he would ever do.

Although Lauren wouldn't be a permanent fixture in William's life, right now she was exactly what he needed. She handled the chip on Will's shoulder the way she handled everything else, with composure and grace. She'd taken him under her care and truly connected with him, treating him with patience and respect. She'd made more progress breaking down the shell of toughness in four days than he'd made in two months.

He cranked the car and pulled from the parking lot. More than once, he'd questioned the wisdom of coming to Ridgely. But this move was turning out to be the best thing for both of them, all because of the addition of Lauren in their lives. He hoped to be able to return the kindness she'd shown.

She was obviously taking comfort in not being

alone. His dog had saved her life once, maybe twice, depending on what her intruder had planned Friday night. If given the opportunity, Zack would do everything in his power to keep her safe.

He wasn't law enforcement. He didn't even own a gun.

But if it meant protecting her, he would put himself in the path of danger in a heartbeat.

SIX

Lauren swung open the Mustang's passenger door. Instead of Kat's house, Zack had stopped in her own driveway. He needed to take Ranger out and feed him lunch. Lauren had texted Kat to let her know they'd be along shortly.

As she approached the house, barks interspersed with howls came from the other side of the front door. "It sounds like Ranger's scolding us for leaving him alone."

"That's his I'm-so-happy-to-see-you-you've-been-gone-forever bark."

Lauren laughed, sliding her key into the lock. As soon as she opened the door, Ranger bounded past her and down the porch steps. He made several circles in the front yard, ears bouncing, before stopping to lift his leg against the oak tree near the edge. Lauren waited on the porch while Zack gave the dog a few more minutes to expel his energy.

"Okay, goofball. Back inside."

The dog sprinted toward the porch and then stopped to look back at Zack.

"Yes, you have to go in. We'll be back in a little while."

Ranger tilted his head to one side and then the other. The long ears and saggy jowls made him look jovial and a bit silly, but the alert eyes seemed to indicate that he understood every word his master said.

When they were inside the car again, Lauren directed Zack to Kat's place five minutes away. As they stepped onto the porch, enticing aromas seeped from the house. Lauren gave two soft knocks and opened the door without waiting for her friend.

When she stepped inside, the scents hit her full-force. "Man, that smells good."

Kat swept into the room. She'd traded the blouse she'd worn to church for a T-shirt, which currently had a couple of reddish splatters on the front.

"Nothing fancy, just my homemade chili."

Soon they were seated around the table, a tossed salad, some dressing choices and a pot of chili in the center. When the meal was dished up and blessed, Kat pointed her spoon at Zack, sitting across the table from her. "I know you're Lauren's new tenant from LA, or you were until last Tuesday. I'm curious how you wound up here."

"I had a friend in high school who was from Tiptonville. She hated the city. Every time she talked about her hometown, she made it sound so charming. So when I decided to leave LA, I did a search for apartments near Tiptonville and found Lauren's ad."

"You got the apartment and lost it less than a week later. Bummer."

"Thank goodness, Lauren's giving me a place to stay right now."

Lauren cut in. "You're doing *me* a favor."

Kat tilted her head. "How do you figure that?"

"You know what happened with Lyle and my store being destroyed." Kat was one of those well-wishers who'd stopped by the demolished store the day after the quake. "And I told you about the theft of my laptops. There's some other stuff that's been going on, too."

Lauren filled her in on having her camera bag snatched and being rear-ended on Thursday, as well as the attempted break-in Friday night.

"When the guy snatched my camera bag, I assumed he thought it was a purse or held jewelry or something of value. When the guy rear-ended me, I was sure it was intentional but didn't know what he wanted. But when my laptops were taken last night, we decided someone was after my photos."

Kat's eyes widened, and her eyebrows drew together. "That's crazy. What do they want with your pictures? Not that you're not a talented photographer."

"I don't know. I'm sure Lyle was involved, since he was in my store that day, but we haven't figured out what these guys want with me. I thought maybe they were some of Lyle's old associates bent on revenge, but why would they still be after me with Lyle gone?" She frowned. "We're hoping these pictures will shed some light on the situation."

As soon as they'd finished lunch, Zack helped Lauren clear and wipe the table and then excused himself to use the restroom.

Kat retrieved her laptop from the living room. As she laid it on the table, she released a slow whistle, letting her gaze trail toward the hall. "That is one hot guy. And he seems really nice. Dare I hope there's some romance in the works?"

Lauren frowned. "You know my situation."

"I do, and it's not a reason to avoid relationships."

"I'll never be able to have children."

"Zack already has a child."

"He's his nephew. He wants children of his own."

"You don't know that."

"Yes, I do. He said so. Face it. I left my future on the operating table that day." She winced at the self-pity that had entered her tone.

Kat crossed her arms. "You're not the only one on the planet who can't have children."

"The cancer gene I carry is a ticking time bomb. I'm clear now, but it could show up anywhere in my body without warning. I can't saddle a man with that kind of uncertainty."

"All of life is uncertain."

"People don't take on uncertainty when they have a choice. Look at my dad. Look at Darren."

Her throat tightened. All she'd ever wanted was a loving husband and a house full of children. Though she'd accepted her situation and stopped asking God "why" a long time ago, allowing her thoughts to linger there too long always put a sickening lump in her stomach.

Before Kat could offer another argument, a door opened down the hall. Lauren held a finger in front of her lips. "Shh, he's coming back."

When Zack reappeared, Lauren took a seat in front of the computer. Zack sat next to her, with Kat on the end. Lauren signed in to her cloud storage and several folders displayed, the most recent titled "Park Pictures" and last Tuesday's date.

She double clicked on the folder. When a bunch of thumbnails appeared, she scrolled to the bottom. "I'll bring these up in the order I took them."

She clicked on the first one, and the image filled the screen. A squirrel sat under an oak tree, an acorn held between its front paws. Next was a female cardinal on a branch.

"See, I told you I take scenery and animal pictures."

There was a picture of a woman walking her dog, and then several where she had zoomed in on the animal, maybe a beagle mix. She'd shot a variety of other photos as she'd walked around the park. The pictures were good—contrast, depth, interesting composition, balance between negative and positive space—but they weren't worth stealing.

She closed the current picture and opened another. "These next few, I shot at a distance with a telephoto lens. A boy was standing near the fountain feeding the birds. They kept swooping down, and I was trying to catch them against the backdrop of the spraying water."

"You were successful in several of them."

She was pleased. She'd captured the boy with his arm raised, tossing bread into the air, birds with their wings spread wide, drops of water glistening in the sunlight.

Zack held up a hand. "Wait a minute. Zoom in. Drag the photo over so you can see the left-hand edge."

She did as he'd instructed. At the side of the frame, she'd captured two men. The taller one wore khakis and a blue polo and stood in profile, brown hair lying in soft layers. The other, shorter but much stockier, faced her fully. He was dressed in jeans and a black T-shirt, his dark hair cut close to his head. Both wore sunglasses.

An icy chill washed through her, an uneasy sense of recognition. She clicked the plus to zoom in and pointed at the screen. "I think this shorter guy is the one who's been after me. I couldn't see my would-be abductor's face because he was wearing a ski mask, but he was short and stocky like this. The man who took my camera bag, I just saw from behind as he was running away, but he had the same build. I watched the guy who ran me off the road walking toward me in my side mirror. He wore a buzz cut and his face was roundish like this. Same with the guy who broke in last night." She looked at Zack. "I'm sure this is the guy."

She shifted her gaze back to the screen. She couldn't see the man's eyes behind the sunglasses. Had he watched her as she'd stood at the other end of the park and snapped his picture?

"What about the other guy?"

At Zack's question, she turned her attention to the taller man. "It's hard to tell, since I caught him in profile, but I don't recognize him."

"Let's check the rest of the pictures."

She nodded and brought up the next photos. She'd finished with the birds at the fountain and had gone back to shooting other parts of the park. As they studied the pictures, nothing stood out.

Soon, there were only five thumbnails left. She clicked on the first.

Zack leaned closer. "You went back to photographing the fountain."

"Yeah. The woman there with her little boy, she's a customer of mine."

The men were gone. By that point, even the boy with the bread had walked away. Little Oliver stood on the short wall that surrounded the fountain, hands raised to catch the spray, his mother's arms wrapped around him.

"I could hear Oliver's laughter and wanted to capture the expression on his face. So I snapped several pictures, gradually moving closer. For the final one, I stepped to the side of the fountain. I planned to print the picture and give it to his mom."

She double clicked the last thumbnail, and the image filled the screen. Her attempt was a success. The boy's expression was one of pure delight—mouth open in a broad smile as he leaned into the overspray.

But Lauren's focus didn't remain on the boy for long. The different angle had captured two men standing about twenty feet beyond where he played.

Zack held up a hand. "Wait."

She was already going for the plus sign. The image grew as she clicked. The taller man was back. She'd captured him in profile again. He was grasping a younger man by the arm. Was it a friendly gesture? Or was he threatening him?

Even in the shadow cast by the bill of his cap, the young man was disturbingly familiar—blond hair sticking out below the cap, mildly shaggy; slim build beneath clothes that fit him a bit too loosely. As she zoomed in, his features became clearer.

She flopped back in the chair. "That's Lyle. I took the picture thirty minutes before he came into my store."

"We need to get this to the police."

She nodded, the gravity of the situation pressing down on her. She'd witnessed something and captured it on camera. And she'd been caught. Whatever she'd seen, it had put her life in danger. There was only one way out of the mess she was in—identify the two unknown men in the photos.

Zack had hoped the pictures she'd taken would provide answers to their questions. Instead, they'd raised even more questions.

Who was the tall guy, and what deal was he making with the shorter man? What kind of disagreement was he having with her brother?

And the most disturbing question of all, since they knew she had captured their transactions on camera, how far were they willing to go to destroy the evidence and make sure she didn't talk?

* * *

Lauren dried the pan she'd used to fry eggs and slid it into the drawer under the range. After taking seconds on Kat's chili, neither she nor Zack had been hungry when dinnertime had arrived, so they'd opted for breakfast fare. William had claimed he was starving but loved eggs and toast, so he had no complaints.

She was still feeling shaken over the photos. But the last one confirmed what she'd suspected—the man in the khakis and polo had been holding something over Lyle. Maybe he'd threatened to hurt him if he didn't do what he was told. Or maybe he'd threatened to hurt her. She hoped the police would figure it out. If the men had an arrest record, it would give the authorities somewhere to start.

Lyle had had all the answers. If he would have just come to her, they could have puzzled it out together, pulled Danny and others in to help. Then maybe Lyle would still be alive and she wouldn't have dangerous men after her.

By tomorrow morning, the photos would be in the hands of investigators. Maybe they were already there. Before leaving Kat's house, she'd called Danny and told him what they'd discovered. He'd asked her to email them to him, saying someone would be on it ASAP.

When she and Zack walked into the living

room, William stood facing one wall. It was her picture wall, with a couple dozen framed photos of friends and family.

Lauren stepped up beside him, and he pointed at one of the pictures. "Is that your brother?"

Was. She didn't correct him aloud. She still caught herself using present tense when she thought of him. More than once, she'd thought of something she wanted to say the next time she saw him. Then realization had slammed into her so hard it had almost left her breathless. It would take time to fully digest the fact that he was gone.

"He sort of looks like you."

Yeah, the resemblance had always been strong. They'd had the same wispy blond hair, the same green eyes, even the same shape to their mouths. A lump swelled in her throat. It would be a long time before she could think of him without feeling a gaping hole in her heart.

"Did you get along?"

"Most of the time. When we were kids, we fought like brothers and sisters do." Some of those fights had extended into adulthood. "Even when I wanted to strangle him, I still loved him."

"Did he love you back?"

She smiled. The honesty and openness of kids. Adults could learn a thing or two from them.

"Yeah, he did." Whenever she'd reach the point that she was ready to throw up her hands and leave him to his own devices, he'd say or do something that would melt her heart.

"Then why did he come in your store with a gun and ski mask?"

Zack cleared his throat behind them. "That's enough with the questions."

Lauren looked at him over one shoulder. "It's okay. I don't mind." She turned back to William. "I think he got hooked up with some bad men and didn't have a choice. They probably threatened him, maybe even said they'd hurt me if he didn't do what they said."

A few feet away, Zack took a seat on the couch. She really didn't mind William's questions. Somehow, sharing with the kid felt good.

William moved to another photo. "Is that your mom?"

The picture he pointed out was of the three of them, the last professional one they'd had made. She'd been sixteen, Lyle thirteen. A few weeks later, their mom's cancer had returned with a vengeance. Fourteen months after that, she'd lost the battle.

"Yeah."

"Does she live here?"

"No, she's gone."

William's gaze met hers. In the brief span of time that followed, he seemed to be studying her. "Gone, like dead?"

"Yeah."

"Did she die in an earthquake, too?"

"No. She had cancer."

He turned back to the photo wall, but his thoughts didn't seem to be on what he was looking at. In fact, his eyes appeared to be fixed between two of the frames. "My mom was killed in a car accident."

"I'm sorry." She stepped closer to drape an arm across his shoulders. "It's so hard. You'll always miss her, but eventually it doesn't hurt quite so badly."

"Yeah." He was silent for several moments. Then he shrugged. "I'm going to play on my Game Boy."

He walked down the hall and disappeared into his room. Lauren joined Zack on the couch. He looked exceptionally solemn. "Thank you."

"For what?"

"For taking time with William. Being willing to share even when it's painful. You're connecting with him in a way I haven't been able to. His bringing up Sara's accident, that's not something he shares with people."

"We both lost our moms."

"How old were you when your dad left?"

"Seven. Lyle was four."

"And your mom was sick. So you stepped up, taking on the role of mother and father." His eyes were filled with sympathy. But something else, too. Admiration. It resonated with something deep inside her, creating a pull that was hard to resist.

His gaze held hers. "You're pretty incredible. You've had your store and apartment destroyed. You've lost your brother. You've been attacked, more than once. But you still take the time to connect with an angry, hurting boy. Even with everything you've been through, you've still managed to be a bright spot in William's and my life."

He lifted a hand to touch her cheek with the back of his index finger. She closed her eyes, drawing strength from that touch. What would it be like to finally let the walls come down, to connect with someone on a level deeper than friendship, to allow a man access to her heart?

She opened her eyes. No, it wouldn't be fair to herself and it wouldn't be fair to Zack.

"How about if we watch the news?" She picked up the TV remote from the coffee table. She'd heard a few stories about the quake. Some towns had gotten it worse than Ridgely. But there hadn't been any deaths that she'd heard about, other than Lyle's, which might have been from his gunshot wound. She hadn't gotten the autopsy results back yet.

When she tuned to the news, a reporter stood in front of a collapsed home speaking with a couple, the woman holding a baby. The banner across the bottom gave her location—Conran, Missouri, across the Mississippi River, just over the state line. She'd been heading outside with her child when the quake began and had stumbled into the yard as the house had come down.

The scene changed to the front of another home. It appeared undamaged, but crime scene tape stretched across the screen. A reporter stood off to the side with a microphone.

"Behind me, authorities are investigating a possible double murder. A Memphis city commissioner and his wife have been found dead at their vacation home on Reelfoot Lake, a short distance from Tiptonville."

The camera panned to the right where flashing red and blue lit up the darkness. Several police cruisers were there, as well as an ambulance and a county crime scene vehicle.

The camera swept back to the reporter, who related that the city commissioner, Samuel Kerman, and his wife, Beverly, had left Memphis on Tuesday morning with plans to return around noon Sunday. Although they'd let family know they were safe after the quake, they'd never made it home. After a call from their daughter, a neighbor had made the grisly discovery.

Lauren shook her head. "That's only twenty minutes from here." Of course, Zack already knew that since he'd been to Tiptonville to get their subs. "This is disturbing. We never have murders in this area."

A grainy video appeared on the screen, captured from a neighbor's security camera. An instant sense of familiarity brushed Lauren's mind. The quality was poor. The subject had been too far away, passing through the camera's line of sight briefly before disappearing.

A second video showed him walking in the opposite direction, reversing his original path. Before disappearing from the frame, he turned, looking almost directly at the camera. The station paused the footage, creating a blurry still.

Lauren gasped and clutched Zack's forearm. The stocky build. The roundish face. Hair in a buzz cut.

"It's him." She whispered the words. "I'm almost positive that's the guy I photographed in the park. I'm hoping the sheriff's tech people will be able to clean up the security image."

The journalist ended his story by calling on the public to contact authorities if they had any information.

Lauren slumped against the cushions at her back, a block of ice settling in her core. The man in the video had met with someone in the park the day of the earthquake. Did the murder of the commissioner and his wife have anything to do with that meeting? Was the tall guy somehow involved? Had he possibly put out a hit on the commissioner and she'd caught it on camera? If so, her photo might be the proof the authorities would need to tie him to the murders.

Now the theft of her camera and computers made sense.

Would the men stop there?

Or would they make sure she didn't live long enough to pass along what she had?

"Wow, it smells good in here."

Zack turned from the griddle to smile at Lauren. She was dressed in black tights and a green T-shirt that brought out the color of her eyes.

"Help yourself. They're hot off the griddle."

He turned back to the counter to use up the last of the batter. Four smaller spoonsful formed mouse ears on two of the pancakes.

A door creaked open and another one closed. William had risen and was in the bathroom. By the time he shuffled into the kitchen, Lauren had dished up her plate and taken a seat at the table.

Zack looked at William over one shoulder. "Good morning, buddy."

Lauren gave her own greeting, in chorus with his, and the boy sank into one of the chairs with a muffled grunt. When Zack put the two special pancakes in front of him, William looked at the plate and stormed from the kitchen. Moments later, his bedroom door slammed shut.

Zack stood frozen. What had just happened?

Lauren's slack jaw and wide eyes showed she was as confused as he was.

She lifted her shoulders in a prolonged shrug. "Maybe he's outgrown Mickey Mouse."

"He didn't think he was too mature six months ago."

"A lot has changed over the past six months. His whole life has been turned upside down."

Zack took a deep breath. Yes, it had. And he had no idea how to help the kid process everything that had happened. For now, he'd give him his space.

He prepared a stack of three pancakes and sat next to Lauren. "I feel like I'm navigating a maze without a map. I never know what will set him off."

"He's got so many emotions swirling around inside, and he doesn't know what to do with them. Maybe making Mickey Mouse pancakes was something special his mom used to do."

"I doubt it. Sara was too busy trying to keep food on the table and a roof over their heads. I tried to help her different times, but although we were close, she was fiercely independent and refused to accept charity. Her life would have been easier if she had."

He nodded toward the fridge where a magnet held a three-by-five index card. It had appeared yesterday. On it, she'd written a Bible verse, something about the God of all comfort comforting people in their troubles so they can comfort others.

"Did you put that there for me?"

"No, for me. But you're welcome to claim it, too."

He could use some comfort, along with patience and wisdom and strength. Because his well of self-sufficiency was rapidly running dry.

He finished the last of his pancakes and stood. "I'm going to try to talk to William."

It didn't go any better than he'd expected. William refused to talk, and Zack wouldn't try to force him. As he stepped back into the hall, the doorbell rang. Every sense shot to high alert. Ranger charged from the kitchen in a flurry of barks and growls.

When Zack peered through the peephole, his tension fled instantly. "It's just Deputy Rutherford."

Lauren swung open the door. "Come on in. You have news?"

"I do."

Ranger settled down immediatcly and wagged his tail. After bending to scratch the furry black-and-tan cheeks, the deputy straightened and faced Lauren.

"We've identified one of the men in your pictures."

"Which one?"

"The shorter, stockier one."

"Have a seat."

Rutherford moved to the love seat, and when she'd eased onto the couch, Zack sat next to her. Ranger lay on the floor between them.

"Who is he?" Instead of resting against the cushion behind her, she was leaning forward, back stiff.

"Edwin Rouse aka Jermaine Thomas and a few other aliases. Over the past thirty years, he's built a rap sheet that spans several states and includes charges from drug trafficking to battery to attempted kidnapping. He's currently wanted in connection with an execution-style killing in Nashville."

Lauren nodded. "Any connection to Memphis?"

"Not that we know of at this point."

"What about the taller man?"

"We're still working on him."

She frowned. "I might have taken a picture of him putting out a hit on the commissioner."

"It's possible, since the man he was with appears to be the one that was caught on the neighbor's security camera. We're hoping to get the image cleaned up enough for a definitive ID."

"That would be helpful." She paused. "The guy who attacked me wasn't working alone. When my brother told him to let me go, he said, 'You take your orders from *us*,' plural. I just don't know what Lyle's connection was."

"We're hoping to learn more in the coming days." Rutherford pushed himself to his feet. "I'll keep you posted on any new developments. In the meantime, be careful." He shifted his gaze to Zack. "I'm glad you're with her, but I'd feel better if she was somewhere far away from here."

"I know." He slid Lauren a glance. "We've had that conversation."

"Units are driving by on a regular basis, but still."

Lauren stood and walked with Rutherford to the door. Instead of opening it, she rested her hand on the jamb, eyebrows drawn together. "I've wondered why the man wanted to abduct me. What if he was trying to force Lyle to do something big—like carry out a hit on the commissioner? Lyle was never violent. There's only one way they could have coerced him to do something like that—threaten my life. What better way to do that than to hold me somewhere?"

Zack shook his head. "If the guy wanted Samuel Kerman killed, why not have the other guy do it to begin with? He obviously has no qualms about killing someone in cold blood."

Lauren shrugged. "I don't know. Maybe they were having Lyle prove his loyalty, especially since he took off and came here when he got out of prison."

Rutherford stepped onto the porch and turned

back around to face Lauren. "Keep your alarm set, and don't go out alone."

As he headed down the stairs toward his car, Lauren closed the door and armed the alarm. She was right. They needed to learn the identity of the unknown man in the photo.

Who would stand to gain from Samuel Kerman's death? Or did someone have a vendetta against the man? People in politics often made powerful enemies. Was that what had happened? Had someone been unhappy with a vote and decided to take vengeance?

And the biggest question of all—at this point, what did they want with Lauren?

SEVEN

Zack pulled into Lauren's driveway and killed the engine. He'd left work just seven minutes ago. He wasn't making near the salary that he had in California, but the short drive with almost zero traffic was a definite plus.

He opened the door, triggering the high-pitched tone of the alarm, which Lauren was now keeping armed around the clock. When he stepped inside, the lamp on the end table was on. She was sitting sideways on the couch, legs stretched out and her back against the arm, an open book in her hands.

He punched in the code, closed the door and rearmed the system. "You're still up."

"I am." She closed the book and swung her feet to the floor.

"How has William been?"

"Moody. Irritable. Withdrawn."

He'd been afraid of that. After the scene at breakfast, he'd been out of sorts the rest of the morning. When Zack had made him accompany them to the bank for Lauren to open the safe-deposit boxes, he'd pouted the entire time. But there'd be no more staying home alone.

At lunchtime, Lauren had made tomato soup and cheese sandwiches. Though William had refused the soup, she'd finally talked him into eating a sandwich. When he'd headed to his room with it, Lauren had given her approval before Zack could voice his objections.

He eased onto the couch, next to her. "He wasn't disrespectful to you in any way, was he?" Zack had tried to be patient with the kid's insolence, considering what he'd been through, but he wasn't going to tolerate any behavior that would upset Lauren.

She shrugged. "Not really."

He studied her. There was too much hesitation in that response. "What did he say?"

"It wasn't a big deal."

"Tell me."

She heaved a sigh. "When it was midafternoon and he was still in his room, I asked him to come out back with me to take Ranger out. He refused. I said he'd feel better if he got out and did something. He told me I didn't know anything and to leave him alone."

Zack sprang to his feet. "I won't tolerate him speaking to you that way. He owes you an apology."

Lauren grabbed his arm and pulled him back down onto the couch. "Give him time. He's had a lot to process. That happens in stages. He'll open up eventually."

He sank back onto the couch. That "opening up" was more likely to happen with her than with him.

His ringtone interrupted his thoughts, and he pulled his phone from his pocket. "Spam risk" was displayed on the screen. He swiped to reject the call, and the time and date displayed once again. The time was no surprise. It was the date that made him feel as if a boulder had been dropped on him. No way could they already be that far into the month.

He laid the phone down and put his head in his hands. "Today would have been my sister's thirtieth birthday."

Lauren released a heavy sigh. "Oh, man. No wonder William was so moody. Special days are tough. For William, his mother's birthday passed without anyone acknowledging it."

Zack flopped back on the couch, letting his hands fall to his lap, palms up. "I feel horrible."

She put her hand in one of his and gave it an encouraging squeeze. "Hey, when is the last time you wrote the date on anything?"

"A week ago last Thursday, when I filled out my new hire paperwork."

"See? You didn't forget Sara's birthday. You just didn't know what day it was until you noticed it on your phone."

He turned to look at her without releasing her hand. It felt good in his, so warm, tiny but strong.

"You're amazing, you know that? With everything you're dealing with, most people would have a hard time looking beyond their own circumstances. But instead of focusing on your problems, you're always offering encouragement to others." And boy, did he need it, more than he'd ever needed anything. He didn't just need that encouragement. He needed Lauren.

She smiled. "I'm not that amazing. I've just learned some lessons over the years. After my mom died, I went through some other tough times. I put on a good act, attended church, said all the right things. But deep down, I was angry at God. After several months of that, I decided that I could spend the rest of my life being bitter, or I could focus on God's goodness and find joy that I can spread to others."

"You certainly do that." He gave her hand another squeeze. "You told me about your relationship with your brother. My home life was totally different from yours. I had both parents, and they're still happily married after thirty-six years. But like you, I was the older child with a sibling who seemed dead set on self-destruction."

He drew in a deep breath and released it in a sigh. "Sara and I were two years apart, and she was determined to not follow in my footsteps. She called me a Goody Two-shoes. Every decision she made seemed to be based on what I *wouldn't* do."

He shook his head. "I wasn't trying to be a Goody Two-shoes. I just always wanted to make decisions I wouldn't regret later. Life was easier that way."

Lauren released his hand and tucked her hair behind her ear. "Based on what you've told me, she must have gotten straightened out."

"She did. At sixteen, she was running with the wrong crowd, smoking weed and choosing loser boyfriends. Then she found out she was pregnant, which settled her down almost overnight. That was when the two of us started to grow into a close relationship."

"William was a blessing. He still is."

Her words hit him right between the eyes. He loved his nephew, and he'd spent a lot of nights agonizing over his bad choices, but he hadn't thought of him as a blessing.

"I guess I haven't yet found the good in this situation."

"Sometimes it isn't obvious until much later. That's when we can look back at the fork in the road and appreciate the side we ended up on. If Lyle had stayed in Memphis, we would never have gotten close. During the past nine months, I had my little brother back, the person he was before Mom got sick and he went off the deep end and I became a killjoy who didn't want him to have any fun."

"I'm glad you were able to connect before it was too late."

He could relate to what she'd said about forks. The decision to come to Ridgely was definitely a fork in the path of his life. Would he eventually be able to look back and see the move as a blessing?

"People weren't happy that I took him in, but I felt it was his only hope. A couple of months earlier, he'd gotten jumped by some inmates and badly beaten. He turned his life over to God after that, but I knew if he stayed in Memphis, around the same bad influences, he'd be back in trouble in no time. So I brought him here."

That sounded exactly like something she'd do. Lauren—encourager of the downcast, comforter of the hurting, mender of broken hearts. "Sara was never in trouble with the law. She was a good person and a loving mother. But she should have dumped the boyfriend. She could have met and married someone who would have been a true father to William. Instead, she stuck with the bio dad, allowing him to constantly slip in and out of their lives. Now William has neither parent. He's angry and broken, and I'm left picking up the pieces."

He lifted his hands and let them fall. "Of everyone on the planet, I'm the least qualified for this job. If you ask William, no matter what I do, it's the wrong thing."

"Hey, come on." She twisted to face him and draped an arm over his shoulder, pulling him into a one-armed hug. "You're doing a wonderful job. There aren't many single men who'd take on the responsibility you have. That's why there are so many people raising their grandkids."

"Mom and Dad offered, but I couldn't do that to them. Dad's having health problems, and they're working through their own grief."

"So, you stepped up, even though it completely upended your life. See? I'm not the only one in this room who's amazing."

The admiration and encouragement in her eyes pushed back his doubts and bolstered his sagging self-esteem. "Thank you."

He returned the hug, encircling her with both arms. When her other arm came up to wrap around him, he tightened his embrace.

Holding her felt so good, so right. The past two months had been too hard—trying to navigate the moods of a troubled teenager who'd just experienced the unthinkable, never able to fully deal with his own grief because he was too busy trying to be that rock for his nephew.

Now Lauren was bearing some of that burden with him. Her open hand moved in slow, soothing circles on his back, her support like salve on the tattered pieces of his soul. He needed a woman like Lauren in his life. William needed Lauren in his life.

He buried his face in her silky blond hair and drew in a slow, deep breath. She'd used some kind of strawberry-scented shampoo or conditioner. Its pleasant fragrance wrapped around him—subtle yet alluring and totally feminine.

He pressed a soft kiss to the side of her face and then withdrew one arm to trace her lips with his thumb. "Do you have any idea how special you are?"

Her eyes locked with his, warm and filled with emotion. She was feeling it, too, not just the pull of attraction, but a connection on a much deeper level.

His gaze dropped to her lips, slightly parted, and he leaned closer. Just before his mouth brushed hers, she turned away.

"You better take Ranger out."

What?

"He's gone to bed with William. I didn't want to let him out in the dark, so he hasn't been out since about six." She pushed herself to her feet, her body radiating tension. "It's almost midnight, well past bedtime."

She was right. It was late. But that wasn't what this was about.

He should never have tried to kiss her. He'd started to cross that friendship line. What a mistake.

They had a lot in common. They were good for each other. Unless he'd totally misread her, she was attracted to him. And she'd obviously connected with William. But offering encouragement and support on a temporary basis was a far cry from considering a long-term commitment. Was that what was holding her back? If it was, he wouldn't blame her.

When he came in from taking Ranger out, Lauren was already in her room, door closed. After setting the alarm, he held a glass to the dispenser in the refrigerator door, and his gaze swept over the index card. He'd read it enough times he could probably quote those verses verbatim. He even knew the reference—II Corinthians 1:3-5.

This time, the last line jumped out at him, is if written in neon, the part about comforting others with the comfort received from God. That was exactly what Lauren was doing.

He'd been wrong. Religion wasn't a crutch, something for the weak. Lauren's faith made her strong enough to comfort others in the midst of her own pain.

He finished his water and walked to the bathroom. The face that stared back at him from the mirror had aged five years in the past two months. Fine lines fanned outward from the corners of his eyes. Vertical creases had taken up permanent residence between his eyebrows, and frown lines framed his mouth.

Lauren's way was working so much better than his. She'd found the comfort promised in those verses. So had his parents.

God, I'm tired of doing this on my own.

He'd posed his questions—why God had taken Sara, why He'd left William orphaned, why God had allowed his life to spin completely out of control. All the whys were no longer important. The only question that mattered now was how he could experience that peace and comfort for himself.

It would begin with repentance. Confession and receiving God's forgiveness. He'd shut Sara down, but he'd still heard.

Doubt crept in. *After I've ignored You for thirty-two years, do You even still want me?*

Something told him God's answer was an unequivocal yes.

"I'd better get to work." Zack rose from the kitchen table the following day. "Thanks for lunch."

William had finished and was in his room with Ranger. The boy was almost back to normal. Yesterday's anger had faded, but a lingering sadness remained.

First thing this morning, Zack had apologized

for forgetting his mom's birthday. He hadn't made excuses, which had raised him up even further in her eyes. He'd also told her that after she'd gone to bed last night, he'd had a long conversation with God. Already he seemed more at peace.

Lauren rose and followed him to the door. A while ago, he'd phoned his parents in California using video chat. After letting William catch up with them, Zack had called her over and introduced her to them. They were warm and friendly and told her they'd been praying for her. She loved them already. That didn't help her in her attempts to resist Zack.

Last night, she'd almost let him kiss her. What had she been thinking? Since then, there'd been a slight awkwardness between them. Nothing overt, just a tense undercurrent in their interactions.

Stepping over the friendship line would be a huge mistake. It didn't matter how badly she wanted to do just that. When Zack decided he couldn't let go of his dream of having children of his own or deal with the uncertainty of never knowing when she might receive a dreaded diagnosis, he'd walk away and the friendship would be over, too.

Zack opened the door and stepped onto the porch. "You're keeping the alarm set, right?"

"Except for when I let Ranger out. Even then,

I look to make sure no one's in the backyard before I open the door."

She locked the door and reset the alarm. Learning about Rouse hadn't made her feel any better. It had only underscored the danger she was in.

When she turned around, William stood facing her photo wall. She'd found him here several times. Something about the pictures seemed to draw him. Maybe they brought up cozy feelings of family.

She stepped up beside him. "Would you like to frame one of the pictures of your mom and hang it here?"

"I already have one in a frame."

He hurried to his room and returned a half minute later with an eight-by-ten wooden frame clutched to his chest. He turned it toward her. The glass was missing and the photo had a couple of nicks, but nothing that detracted from the subjects. William looked to be about nine or ten. Behind him, a woman with Zack's dark hair and blue eyes stood with her chin resting on the top of his head, her arms wrapped around his chest.

She'd seen the photo albums when Zack had pulled them from the debris. She'd apparently been tied up when they'd recovered this one.

"That's a great picture. I can see she really loved you."

"Uncle Zack said he's going to buy a new piece of glass to go in here, but he hasn't done it yet."

"We'll make sure that happens this week, no matter what. In the meantime, what do you think of hanging that picture right here?" She pointed to a space next to one of her and Lyle.

"That would be awesome."

Lauren went to the kitchen and fished around in her junk drawer until she found a hammer and nail. Soon William's photo hung on the wall with all of hers.

As William stood staring at it, sadness seemed to settle in his eyes. "I'm afraid people are going to forget her." His gaze went to his feet. "Uncle Zack did."

"No, sweetie, he didn't forget. He just didn't know what day it was. As soon as he saw the date on his phone, he knew right away that it was your mom's birthday."

He pressed his lips together. "I'm afraid that when I get old, I'm gonna forget what she looks like."

"No, you'll never forget. She'll always be right here." Lauren planted a fist against her heart. "Any time you want to feel her close, hold her picture."

She moved over and lightly touched one of the framed photos. "A friend took this on one of my mom's rare days off. We had a picnic at Reel-foot Lake State Park. It was a really good day." She looked at the image behind the glass. She and Lyle were sitting on top of one of the picnic tables, their feet dangling over the edge. Their mom was on the bench next to them, the park's pavilion in the background to the left. "When I look at this, I think about how much my mom loved me. Pictures help us remember."

She looked over at William, so quiet and solemn, then gave his shoulder a little shake. "Hey, you know what I like to do on my mom's birthday?"

"What?"

"Buy a chocolate cake and eat the whole thing by myself."

He lifted his eyebrows, a smile quivering at the corners of his lips. "You do?"

"It might take me a few days, but I don't share it with anybody."

"Can we do that today?"

She hesitated. After the events of the weekend, she hadn't planned to go anywhere. Rouse was out there gunning for her—and they didn't know who the other man in her photos was.

"Your uncle would be really upset at us."

"He doesn't have to know."

"It's not good to keep secrets from the people we love."

"Even if it's to keep from upsetting them?"

How was she supposed to answer that? "I have an idea."

She picked up her phone and scrolled to her

contacts. After choosing Danny Rutherford's name, she pressed the blue text icon.

Protection probably wouldn't be needed, not in a public place in broad daylight. Especially with a sheriff's deputy standing by. But she asked for an escort anyway.

Ten minutes later, a white cruiser pulled into the driveway, Lake County Sheriff in green letters on the sides. She let the blinds fall back into place. "Deputy Rutherford is here."

After resetting the alarm, Lauren followed the boy and dog onto the porch. She waved at Danny and ushered her two passengers into the blue Jeep. She'd be keeping it for at least another two weeks while work was completed on her own. The adjuster had called that morning to let her know he'd declared her vehicle repairable.

Danny backed into the road, and she pulled out in front of him. All the way to Tiptonville, he maintained a steady distance behind her. When she reached Food Rite, she pulled into the center aisle and selected a space halfway down. The white cruiser moved past in her rearview mirror.

William turned around in his seat. "Where's he going?"

"He'll probably circle the lot, looking for anyone suspicious."

Lauren climbed from the Jeep. William and Ranger bounded around the front, the dog wearing his vest, his leash in William's hand. Together they walked into the store and, after snagging a cart, headed straight for the deli and bakery.

Several cakes were displayed with the donuts and other goodies on the tables lined up there. She read the labels on each of the plastic covers—strawberry, lemon streusel, triple chocolate fudge, honey bun. She moved to the cooler at the end where several more cakes waited inside.

William peered through the glass. "Carrot cake. That was Mom's favorite." She removed it from the cooler and stepped to the counter. "Any chance you could write 'Happy Birthday, Mom' in orange frosting on top?"

The employee smiled at them. "Absolutely. Give me a few minutes."

"Thank you." She looked at William. "What do you want for dinner tonight?"

William thought for a moment. "Corndogs."

Lauren lifted her eyebrows. The kid could pick anything he wanted and he chose corndogs?

"And hamburgers tomorrow night."

William's choice for two meals to celebrate his mom's birthday. Nothing wrong with that. "Okay. Let's go find some."

When they got back to the bakery counter with the cart loaded, the cake was decorated and packaged for them to take home.

As they were leaving the checkout, Lauren's phone buzzed with an incoming text. She pulled it from her purse. It was Danny. He had to respond to a call. She frowned at his instructions to stay inside until he got back. Both the Angus burgers and the corndogs would be thawed long before she arrived home.

She stepped outside and scanned the parking lot. The cruiser was moving up the center aisle toward her. Danny eased to a stop, and she hurried to his open driver's window.

"I've got frozen stuff that I need to get home. We'll be careful." She smiled down at the dog. "Besides, we've got Ranger."

Danny frowned. "What if someone follows you?"

"I'll have William call 9-1-1 the moment we notice anything suspicious. When we get close to Ridgely, we'll call the nonemergency number and have someone follow us the rest of the way."

She was probably going overboard. No one had bothered her since Saturday night's break-in. Maybe they had what they wanted and wouldn't come back. A trickle of uncertainty crept over her, but she shoved it aside.

Danny heaved a sigh of resignation. "I'll watch you walk to the Jeep. Then lock yourself inside."

She gave him a salute. "Will do."

While they hurried to her vehicle, Danny drove down the next aisle and circled around to come up behind her. She pressed the button on her key fob and swung open the Jeep's back door.

"Can I hold Mom's cake?"

"Sure."

While she loaded the other items, William told Ranger to hop into the back. Then he slid into the front passenger's seat and held out his hands. As she passed him the plastic container, he put one hand flat on the bottom and wrapped his other arm around the circumference as if he were guarding something precious.

She closed his door and glanced around the parking lot. There were less than a dozen vehicles parked. All were empty except a Ford pickup truck. A middle-aged man stepped from behind the wheel and walked toward the store.

Lauren lifted a hand and waved Danny on. She'd held him up long enough. All she had to do was wheel the cart into the corral one aisle over and get in the Jeep. Nothing would happen during that brief period of time.

The sheriff cruiser pulled from the parking lot and traveled south down Everett Street. As she rolled the cart toward the corral, Danny made a left, headed toward 78. In spite of her silent reassurances, the moment he disappeared from view, an overwhelming sense of vulnerability descended on her—the feeling she was being watched.

She shoved her cart between the curved metal railings, letting it crash into the two already there. She needed to get back to the Jeep and lock herself inside ASAP.

Somewhere nearby, an engine revved. She spun toward the sound as a beige sedan shot from the grain storage facility across the street and into the Food Rite parking lot. She raced toward the Jeep as the car bore down on her. She'd never make it.

Changing direction, she ran back toward the store. The vehicle raced past. Tires squealed as the driver braked hard, wheels turned sharply to the right. The car came to a stop sitting parallel to the building, right in front.

The sedan's passenger door swung open, and the stocky man she now recognized jumped out. Still at a full run, she veered away from him. A short distance to the right of Food Rite was a Tae Kwon Do studio. Family Dollar and Dollar Tree were on the far end. Other shops were nestled in. If she could make it into one of those stores, maybe her assailants wouldn't follow.

She'd just leaped over the curb in front of the karate studio when someone slammed into her from behind. She came down hard against the concrete, sliding on her elbows and forearms.

Before she could spring back to her feet, arms wrapped around her waist like bands of steel, and her assailant slung her over his shoulder.

She screamed and kicked but was no match for his strength. The sedan had moved forward. The man who held her swung open the back door.

"Hey, put her down."

Lauren twisted toward the voice with a heavy Southern accent. An elderly man had just come out of Food Rite and was hobbling in their direction. He lifted his cane in the air and shook it. "Put her down, or I'm calling the cops."

Lauren's chest clenched. *God, please don't let anyone get hurt.*

As her gaze swept across the parking lot, she almost collapsed in relief. Ranger was charging toward her, his legs a blur. William was about fifteen feet behind him running full speed.

The man who held her lowered her to her feet. As he tried to shove her into the back seat of the sedan, she pressed her right foot against the door jamb. A hand wrapped around her ankle as a second on her back forced her to bend over.

Suddenly, there was a high-pitched scream right behind her. The next instant, she was free.

She leaped to the side and spun. The old man was about fifteen feet away and still advancing, cane raised overhead, clutched in both hands. William was a little farther back, running as fast as his legs could carry him.

Ranger was right behind her assailant, teeth sunk into the back of the man's thigh. He tried to slap the dog away, but Ranger held on.

The old man reached them and brought his cane down hard on her would-be abductor's head. He squealed again and dove headfirst into the back seat. Ranger either released him or lost his grip. Probably the latter. When the car squealed away, a jagged piece of bloody denim lay on the asphalt.

When she looked back at the sedan, it was at the other end of the shopping plaza, making a sharp right to leave the parking area. It was too far away to get a tag number.

"Are you okay, young lady?"

She looked at the man who'd come to her aid. Her forearms stung where the concrete had rubbed off several layers of skin, and one of her knees felt badly bruised. "I am now. Thank you for your help." She shifted her gaze to William. "And thanks for getting Ranger out."

"I heard the car roaring up behind us and saw you running. So me and Ranger jumped out and ran up to the building. When Ranger saw what was happening, he charged ahead and sank his teeth into the guy like he was Cujo or something." He looked toward the Jeep. "I think the doors are still open."

"No problem. I'm glad you acted so quickly." She looked at the elderly man. "You didn't have a chance to call 9-1-1, did you?"

"I don't have no cell phone. Don't have service out where I live."

"But you—" She smiled. When he'd threatened to call the police, he'd been bluffing. Her assailant had had more to fear from the cane than the nonexistent cell phone.

After hurrying to the Jeep to retrieve her purse, she rejoined William, Ranger and the old man in front of the karate studio, which was currently closed. She placed her call, and the old man, who introduced himself as Wilbur Jennings, agreed to stay as a witness.

Five minutes later, a Tiptonville police cruiser pulled into the parking lot, and an officer approached them.

After Lauren had relayed the events of the afternoon, Mr. Jennings corroborated everything she said, including how he'd hit the man with his cane. The officer made notes as they talked.

"Did you notice what kind of car it was?"

Lauren shook her head. "Just that it was a Chevy. I noticed the bowtie on the front."

"Impala, maybe ten, fifteen years old."

She looked at Mr. Jennings. He made a much better witness than she did.

"Did either of you notice any part of the tag number?"

"Sure did."

Lauren did a double take. "You did?"

"Yep, it was…" He squinted, as if concentrating hard. Then he closed his eyes altogether. "RTB 406."

The officer raised his brows. "You're sure?"

"Yep. I always try to think of ways to help me remember stuff. Like 'round the bend.'"

The officer stopped writing. "What?"

"RTB, round the bend. Like in 'I live over yonder round the bend.' And 406 was my house number when I was a teen."

"All righty then. Tennessee tag?"

"Yep, one of the regular blue ones."

After radioing Dispatch to put out a BOLO for the vehicle, the officer looked at William. "Do you have anything to add?"

"No, sir, I think they said it all." He pointed at the small piece of torn denim lying on the ground. "Did you want to take that?"

The officer smiled. "I'm guessing this is from your dog taking a bite out of the guy."

After retrieving gloves and a plastic bag from his vehicle, he picked up the item. Maybe there were prints or DNA that would provide hard evidence against Rouse.

When the officer was finished with them, Lauren thanked Mr. Jennings again, and she and William walked to the Jeep, Ranger following.

William opened the back door. "Get in, Ranger."

She settled into the driver's seat with a sigh. She owed her life to a dog, a thirteen-year-old kid and an eighty-something-year-old man.

Soon, they were heading south on 78 toward Ridgely. As expected, no one was following her. Since every unit in Lake County was looking for them, the men were likely in hiding.

"Are we going to tell Uncle Zack what happened?"

She glanced over at William. "He'll probably find out. It would be better if he heard it from us first."

"He'll be mad at me."

"No, he'll be mad at *me*."

"But I'm the one who asked if we could get the cake."

Lauren looked over at William. He looked sincerely worried.

"It's okay. I'll take all the blame."

And rightfully so. Going out had been reckless. She should have waited until tomorrow morning, when Zack could accompany them. Instead, she'd put them all in danger, Ranger included.

She was still going to call Ridgely Police to escort her the rest of the way home. After almost getting caught, Rouse wasn't likely to attack her again today.

But it was just a matter of time. He was out there—waiting, watching, planning his next move.

When and how would it happen?

And who else might get caught in the crossfire?

EIGHT

Zack sprang up from the table. "You did what?"

He didn't even try to keep his voice down. So much for slipping in quietly and not disturbing his nephew.

As soon as he'd arrived home, Lauren had offered him a piece of cake. He'd assumed she'd made it or a friend had dropped it by. He'd just finished the piece when she'd lifted her right hand to tuck her hair behind her ear, exposing the underside of her forearm. It looked like she'd taken a trip down an asphalt slide.

Whatever she was getting ready to say, she'd prefaced it with the admission that she and William had gone to Food Rite in Tiptonville. He had a feeling the story was going to get a whole lot worse.

She'd risen when he had and was standing in front of him. He took her hand and held it aloft. "I'm guessing this didn't happen in the dairy aisle."

"No, I was outside and got pushed."

He let her hand fall. "By who?"

She winced, obviously uncomfortable with the direction of the conversation. "The stocky guy in the photos."

"And you somehow thought it was a good idea to go to Tiptonville, knowing that same man is suspected of committing a double murder there?"

"The Food Rite is the nearest grocery store. It's where I always shop. I could have gone to Dyersburg, but that would have been twice the distance. Besides, that murder happened outside of Tiptonville."

She heaved a sigh. "I'm sorry. I took every precaution. Danny followed me over there and waited in the parking lot. But then he got called away."

Zack shook his head. "What was so important that you had to risk your life going to the grocery store?"

"A cake. I thought William needed cheering up, something to honor his mom. I bought her favorite cake and had the associate at the bakery put 'Happy Birthday, Mom' on top."

Zack closed his eyes and tried to calm the exasperation swirling through him. Though he was upset with her actions, he couldn't fault the reasons behind them. Always thinking of others. That was Lauren.

Something horrible could have happened to her this afternoon. The very thought made him sick to his stomach. She'd become an important part of William's and his lives. Although he longed for more, if all Lauren wanted was friendship, he'd take it. Whatever the future held, he didn't want to face it without her in his life.

When she put a hand on his shoulder, he opened his eyes. She was looking up at him, her gaze pleading. "It all worked out. William got to honor his mom, and we made it home safely. God protected us."

"You can't expect God to protect you when you take unnecessary chances. What about 'God helps those who help themselves'?"

"That's not in the Bible."

It's not? "The point is, you can't just throw caution to the wind and assume everything will work out okay."

"I didn't throw caution to the wind. I told you—"

He held up a hand to cut her off. "I know, you took precautions. Please promise me you won't try something like that again."

"I won't."

"So why did the guy push you down? What was he after?"

She winced again and pulled her lower lip between her teeth. Yeah, he *really* wasn't going to like her response to that question.

"He was chasing me and knocked me down." She paused. She was likely trying to figure out how to sugar coat what had happened.

"Come on, spit it out."

"He tried to force me into the back seat of a car." Her words came out in a rush, and his breath stalled in his lungs. She continued, her tone heavy. "If I'd gone alone, things would have turned out differently."

She relayed everything that had happened. "I can't tell you how relieved I was to see Ranger and William running toward me."

Pride swelled in Zack's chest, along with love for both his nephew and his dog. "Ranger isn't trained in police work, but he's always been protective. When someone threatens one of his people, he'll do whatever it takes to defend them."

"Am I one of his people?"

"You are." He could hardly believe it himself. It was one week ago that Ranger had located Lauren in the debris. During that week of being together twenty-four/seven, they'd formed a tight bond. When it came time for William and him to find a new place, the dog wasn't going to be happy.

"He was worth his weight in gold today. Thanks to Ranger, the Tiptonville Police Department currently has a bloody piece of denim in evidence."

"I'll have to give him some extra treats."

"I also had help from an old man with a cane, somebody that was shopping at Food Rite. He came out of the store and charged right for us, waving his cane over his head. My attacker was trying to get Ranger off of him, and before he knew what was happening, the old man had cracked the cane over his head."

"Did you know the older man?"

"Never seen him before. He was just a Good Samaritan." She paused. "The guy who attacked me probably figured taking off with one scrawny woman would be a breeze. He didn't anticipate encountering a protective dog and a feisty old man. I think the cane was the final straw, because that's when he dove into the car and they took off."

They? "Wait a minute. There were two of them?"

"Yeah, someone else was driving."

"Can you identify the other guy?"

"I never saw him. I was too focused on keeping the guy who'd grabbed me from stuffing me into the car."

Zack stalked from the kitchen and began to pace the small living room. He'd already talked to her about leaving the area. More than once. Both times, she'd said she couldn't.

He'd give it another shot. "You need to leave."

"I can't. I've got too much going on here."

"Do you really think these guys are going to give up? They're pretty desperate to attack you in front of a grocery store in broad daylight. The next stop might be right here."

Now it was her turn to pace. Worry creased her features. She was scared. For good reason. He wasn't going to soothe her fears.

"What if one evening when you let Ranger out, one guy keeps him distracted while the other kicks in your door? The dog will be in the backyard, and there won't be any old men with canes. You need to disappear until the police catch these guys and lock them up."

"I don't know where I'd go."

He couldn't even offer any suggestions. He'd never been to this part of the country, didn't know anyone who lived within a thousand miles of here.

Except… "I have an idea."

He didn't know anyone who currently lived here, but he still had contact with his friend from Tiptonville. "Remember, I told you I ended up here because I went to school with a girl who grew up in this area?"

"Yes?" Hope filled her features.

"She told me about an old cabin her aunt and uncle had out in the middle of nowhere. It was rustic, no electric or running water."

She frowned. "Probably doesn't have cell service, either. Being unable to call for help doesn't sound like a good plan."

"I'll get a satellite phone." He took both of her hands in his. "Let's get a hold of some of your law enforcement people and have them come up with a game plan to catch these guys. Then we'll all disappear while they do their thing."

"All of us? What about William's school and your job?"

"School won't start for at least another week, maybe longer. William's a smart kid. He'll catch up if he misses some time. As far as my job, I'll tell them I have a family emergency."

The fewer people who knew about his real reasons for disappearing, the safer Lauren would be. As far as his claim about the family emergency, keeping William safe had reached 9-1-1 status. And Lauren…he would want nothing more than to explore the possibility of the three of them becoming a family. But Lauren had slammed that door shut last night. Not that he blamed her.

She sank onto the couch and clasped her hands in her lap. "All right. I'll get a hold of Danny first thing tomorrow."

"And I'll call my friend Vicki whose family had the cabin."

He had another call to make, too. He hadn't told his parents about any of the threats. He hadn't wanted to worry them. With today's events, that had all changed.

Because now he and Lauren needed those extra prayers too badly.

Lauren pulled a heavy coat from the hall closet and added it to the lighter jacket she'd flipped over the arm of the couch. She'd likely need both. Although it was comfortable now, the first cold spell of the season was headed their way. Before tomorrow morning, it was supposed to dip into the low forties.

Zack had called his friend late last night. The good news was her aunt and uncle still owned the cabin. The bad news was no one had been there in more than a decade, so she didn't know if it was still standing. If it was, they were welcome to it, but they were currently waiting for directions.

A ringtone sounded in the spare bedroom, where Zack and William were packing. Getting ready to leave seemed premature when they didn't have their destination nailed down. It was already noon, but with the two-hour time difference, she hadn't expected early-morning confirmation.

Zack's baritone voice drifted to her from down the hall. Judging from his side of the conversation, this was the call he'd been waiting for. She heard "Jackson" and "Chickasaw State Park." He repeated back a series of directions. Their destination was going to be as remote as she'd suspected.

After ending the call, he walked into the living room. "It's set. We have a place to stay. The bad guys will never find you there."

"I heard Chickasaw State Park."

"Yeah, sounds like we'll be east of there, in

some of those fourteen thousand acres of forest that surrounds the park. That's how Vicki described it, anyway. There's supposed to be a dirt drive going to the cabin, but after all this time, it's probably so overgrown that it's little more than a narrow footpath. I'm not sure my car will manage it."

"You can't take your car." The paint job on that beautiful red Mustang would be destroyed. Besides, they'd probably need a four-wheel drive.

Taking the rental vehicle wasn't an option. First thing this morning, she'd called Danny, who'd gotten with Ridgely and Tiptonville. The three agencies would be working together to nail these guys.

Apparently, one of the detectives with Lake County Sheriff had shoulder-length blond hair and was Lauren's build. She would stay in the house, leaving the blinds open just enough for people to see movement inside. Between the physical resemblance and the Jeep parked in the driveway, anyone watching would believe Lauren was there.

Outside, other law enforcement personnel would take turns doing surveillance with binoculars. Everyone's hope was that the men would make another attempt to abduct her within the next few days. Then law enforcement could move in and apprehend them.

Zack crossed his arms and leaned against the wall. "What we really need is a four-wheeler. Do you know anyone who has one?"

"Several people, but not in that area."

"Someone who might be willing to load it up and follow us down?" Everyone had agreed the Mustang needed to be gone. If the killers thought Zack was there, they'd never make their move.

"Probably. But where would we leave your car?"

"Maybe I can leave it in the parking lot at the park, and we can take the four-wheeler the rest of the way. It sounds like it would only be a few miles."

As Zack headed back to the spare bedroom to finish packing, William emerged carrying one of her cloth shopping bags filled with clothes and personal items. He had the Game Boy clutched in his other hand. He looked up at Lauren as he passed. "Anything you need me to do?"

"Nope, I think we're good."

Since yesterday's attack, he seemed to be viewing the prospect of going into hiding as an adventure. He'd probably change his mind after a few days with no power, running water, TV or internet.

Zack stepped back into the hall. "Do you have air mattresses? I have no idea what the furnishings are like."

"I've got four air mattresses and four sleeping bags."

"Wow, one for each of us."

She grinned. "And Ranger. I sometimes take my Kids Club girls camping, and a couple of them don't have equipment."

"We'll need blankets, too. Several."

"I've already laid them out."

"With the cold temperatures we're going to be getting the next three nights, I'm hoping the fireplace is usable."

The ringtone on her cell phone interrupted their conversation. She snatched it from the coffee table and looked at the screen. It was Danny. After his greeting, he asked how she and Zack were coming on preparations.

"Good. We've got directions to the place and have our personal items and some of our food packed. I still need to get my camping gear out of the shed."

"Camping gear? I thought you were staying in a cabin."

"We are, one that's completely off-grid. We'll stop on our way through Jackson and get several gallons of water and some food that doesn't require refrigeration. Zack is also getting a satellite phone. He wants to make sure he can call out if something happens."

"Good idea."

"Is everyone into position?"

"Yes," Danny said, "As of ten minutes ago."

"I've also got a couple of phone calls to make. I'm going to try to get someone to follow us with a four-wheeler. The dirt road to this cabin hasn't been used in years. We're not sure Zack's Mustang can make it."

"Sounds pretty iffy."

"You haven't heard whether Tiptonville police were able to locate the car from yesterday, have you?"

"They weren't. The tag they ran came back stolen. It was taken off of an older Toyota Tundra."

She sighed. "I'll text you when we're ready to leave."

"Good. Several of us will make sure you're not followed."

Lauren thanked him and set to work on locating a four-wheeler. She struck out on her first call. Her friend was willing to loan it out, but couldn't get away until this evening.

The second friend she called could leave in two hours. Matt owned an older Kawasaki Mule, a four-seater with a small bed on the back, four-wheel drive. Perfect for their purposes. She arranged to meet him at Kroger in Jackson. By the time she and Zack left Ridgely and they made their two stops there, the timing should be perfect.

Less than an hour later, the three of them had loaded everything they'd need into the Mustang's trunk. If there was anything they'd forgotten, they could go back out. More than an hour and a half from home, no one would recognize them.

Lauren pulled out her phone and sent a text to Danny.

Ready to leave.

After his brief confirmation, she headed out the door. She'd given him the house key earlier. Sometime this afternoon, someone would drop off the female detective. If anyone was watching, they'd assume it was Lauren arriving home. That was the plan, anyway.

At Danny's recommendation, he and Zack had checked the Mustang for tracking devices that morning. Her rental was the most likely vehicle for the men to try to track, but it never hurt to be extra cautious. As expected, it was clean.

The trip to Jackson was uneventful, and the stops there went smoothly. Zack acquired a satellite phone, and by the time they walked from Kroger, Matt had pulled into the parking lot with the Mule on a small trailer behind his truck.

Lauren hurried over to talk with him, William and Zack in her wake. Following introductions, they walked away to load the groceries, and she stayed with Matt.

"If you want to head straight to Chickasaw's parking area, we'll make sure we can find this place. Then we'll meet you there at the park. I can't tell you how much I appreciate this."

"I still owe you for helping me pass high school algebra."

She laughed. "I think you paid back that debt a long time ago."

Forty minutes later, they passed the turnoff for Chickasaw State Park. The truck's turn signal came on behind them. Zack pressed the brake and continued down Highway 100.

"We're looking for Lake Loop Road on the right."

Lauren squinted at the street sign ahead as Zack drew closer. "This is it."

He navigated the turn onto the gravel road. "Now we're looking for Cagle Trail on the left."

They'd gone about a mile when they came to an unmarked gravel road.

"This has to be it." Zack made the turn. "Now we're looking for the dirt drive. It's supposed to be about a mile or two ahead on the left. Vicki said there used to be a four-by-four wooden post with a red reflector on top, but it may have rotted and come down over the past ten years."

As they scanned the trees and underbrush beside them, Zack covered what seemed like four miles barely resting on the accelerator. Finally, he braked. "I think we missed it."

After negotiating a three-point turn, he headed back toward the highway.

Lauren held up a hand. "Stop." Right outside her window was a wooden post sticking up twelve or fourteen inches out of the ground, its upper surface jagged where the top had broken off. "I think this is it."

Zack stopped the car. After shifting into Park, he got out and disappeared into the woods. A minute or two later, he returned.

"The Mule should be able to navigate this. Even so, I might be pulling out the hatchet or ax."

Both tools stayed with her camping supplies. She'd brought them to cut firewood.

Thirty minutes had passed by the time they got back to that point with the Mule. The sun was already two-thirds of the way through its descent. They wouldn't have much time to get settled in before dusk.

As they made their way along the overgrown path, small branches slapped at them and vines snagged on their clothing. Finally, the narrow path opened up to a small clearing, dark woods encroaching all around. In the center sat a dilapidated cabin.

Long shadows stretched across it. Stones that had at one time been a chimney were lying in a pile against one side. On the other side, the roof sagged, forming gaps between the cedar shakes. She hoped plywood decking beneath had kept out the majority of the rain. Surprisingly enough, the windows appeared intact; those she could see, anyway. Maybe the inside would be livable.

Either way, she was thankful for what she had. For the first time in more than a week, she was safe. No one would find her all the way out here.

She walked to the back of the Kawasaki. The sun was low in the sky, hidden by the trees. After sliding her arm through the straps of her duffel, she picked up two of the bags they'd gotten from

Kroger. Then she made her way to the cabin, swallowing hard.

Zack had prepared her. She'd known before she left home that the place would be rustic and remote.

Once it got fully dark, it would also be spooky.

A shudder passed through her and she shook off the uneasiness.

She'd watched one too many scary movies that took place in dark woods.

NINE

Lauren walked from the woods into the clearing, dragging two limbs. They were around ten feet long, measuring about five inches in diameter at the largest end. Perfect for firewood.

"Here you go." She parked the limbs next to where Zack was working with the hatchet. The ax was lying on the ground next to him.

Although the chimney outside was nothing but a pile of rocks, an old, wood-burning, cast-iron stove sat at one end of the combination kitchen/ living area, its metal pipe extending through the back portion of the roof.

After arriving late Tuesday afternoon, she and William had spent the last hour of daylight gathering limbs while Zack had cut them into pieces that would fit into the wood compartment of the stove. By the time she'd opened cans of baked beans, Vienna sausages and peaches, Zack had had a roaring fire going and a sizable stack of wood on the side of the stove.

That sizable stack had only gotten them through one-third of the night. As the stove had cooled, so had the cabin. They would have been truly miserable if not for the sleeping bags and extra blankets.

She headed back into the woods. Rustling somewhere to her left told her where William was working. Almost three days had passed since they'd come to the cabin. It was now Friday. If something didn't break soon, they'd be spending the weekend there.

William's view of the experience as an adventure had lasted a day and a half. Now he was just plain bored. Gathering firewood took up two or three hours of his day. That left thirteen or fourteen with no TV, no internet and no friends to talk to. With the Game Boy almost dead and no way to charge it, soon he wouldn't even have that. She should have thought to bring games. Monopoly or Parcheesi or Uno in the light of the lantern would have helped pass time in the evenings.

There was a louder rustle from William's direction, moving rapidly closer. Ranger appeared and ran two circles around her before charging back toward the boy. The dog seemed to be the only one enjoying himself.

She approached Zack with more branches. He'd taken what he'd cut and formed three neat piles. "You're getting quite a stash there."

Last night's had lasted till almost morning.

Though the fire had been gone when they'd gotten up, the stove had still been putting out ample heat.

"I'm getting it figured out. My goal is to have fire left burning when we get up tomorrow morning."

William appeared with a limb large enough that it required him tugging with both hands. Ranger shot past him and stopped next to Lauren, tail wagging and excitement rippling through his body.

William dropped the end of the limb. "Can I take a break? I think Ranger wants to go inside."

Upon hearing his name, the dog barked and his tail wagged harder. Lauren smiled. It was probably the boy rather than the dog who wanted to go in.

"I'm fine with it if your Uncle Zack is."

"Sure. You've worked hard. Lauren and I will be in in about an hour for lunch."

She watched the boy and dog disappear into the cabin. The interior hadn't been nearly as bad as they'd expected. The musty smell had all but disappeared after leaving the doors and windows open for several hours.

Over Zack's objections, she'd given him and William the bedroom, which was furnished with an antique dresser and a full-size bed. They'd stripped off the musty bedding and replaced it with two of the sleeping bags and blankets they'd brought from home. She'd taken the living room couch for herself. It was moth-eaten and dusty, but swept off and covered with a sleeping bag, it was quite comfortable.

Even William had been happy with their accommodations until he'd discovered the restroom facilities consisted of an outhouse at the edge of the woods.

Lauren turned back to Zack. "How about if we take a short break. I'd like to see if Danny has any updates."

He laid down the hatchet and handed her the phone. She navigated to Danny's contact information, which Zack had programmed in before leaving the store. After exchanging greetings, she put him on speaker and asked if he had any news.

"Not yet, but we're working on it. Lake County and Memphis have been working together on the murder of Commissioner Kerman and his wife. The commissioner hadn't received any threats, but there's been a request for a zoning change under consideration for the past couple of months. Borgstrum Developing has been trying to get an area rezoned from R-6 to RU."

Lauren frowned. "English please?"

"Single family to apartments. Seems those middle-class homeowners in the neighborhoods around there don't want a six-story apartment complex in their midst."

"But what does that have to do with Samuel Kerman's murder?"

"The variance may still not pass without his vote," Danny said, "but he's been the most vocal opponent. Also, this Victor Borgstrum apparently has his hands in a lot of different business endeavors, and the authorities believe not all of it is aboveboard. The feds have even come in and looked at his books but haven't found anything they could nail him on."

"Have they been able to tie him to this Rouse, or whatever he's calling himself these days?"

"Not yet."

"This Borgstrum guy, he's not the other man in my photos, is he?"

"Nope. I even pulled up his websites. Your man isn't any of his principals, either."

"Any idea what Lyle's connection might have been with Borgstrum or the guys in the park?"

"'Fraid not. They're working hard on it, though. I get the impression they really want to nail this Borgstrum character on something."

After thanking Danny, she disconnected the call and handed the phone to Zack. "I guess it's back to work. When I was looking for limbs, I came across a downed oak tree. The trunk is probably two feet in diameter, so you won't get through it with the ax, but some of the limbs might be manageable."

Zack laid down the hatchet and picked up the ax. "Show me."

She led him sixty or seventy feet into the

woods and stopped near the vertical mass of exposed roots. "Oak burns slower and cleaner than pine. It's also harder, so it won't split as easily, but you'll be able to keep the fire going longer."

Although dry brown leaves clung to the other hardwoods, this tree had been down long enough that its limbs were bare. Zack moved along the trunk, ducking through and stepping over the larger lower limbs. After bringing the ax down several times, he pulled out what he'd severed. The cut end was a good fourteen inches in diameter.

"If you cut that into logs and quarter them, you'll have some good firewood. Then maybe you'll be up only twice during the night." She gave him a sympathetic smile. "You'll be glad when this is over and you can get some uninterrupted sleep." They'd both been up and down the past three nights feeding the stove.

He dropped the ax and took both of her hands in his. "I'll be glad when this is over because I'll know you're safe."

His gaze held hers, and she couldn't look away. As hard as she'd tried to not fall for him, she'd failed miserably. He was everything she'd ever wanted in a man—kind, compassionate, selfless, someone who cared deeply and didn't hesitate to sacrifice for those he loved.

He squeezed her hands, and a sense of longing swelled inside, so powerful it almost took her breath away. She'd told herself for so long that she was content living alone, that the relationships she had with friends, customers and people at church satisfied her need to connect with others.

On those rare occasions when loneliness crept in and she longed for that special someone to share her life with, she'd vowed to let her relationship with God fill that void. For the past decade, she'd been able to do just that. Why was she struggling so hard now?

God, please help me look at Zack as nothing more than a friend.

But what if God had other plans? What if He'd brought Zack into her life to fulfill the longing of her heart?

She swallowed hard. He stood unmoving, still staring into her eyes, as if waiting for something. Permission? She'd already rejected him once.

Rejecting him was the last thing she wanted to do now. Invisible cords seemed to pull her toward him. Still, he waited. Was he wanting to know that she was sure?

She didn't know herself. All she knew was that right now, she wanted Zack to be a permanent part of her life, didn't want him to ever walk away. She rose up on her tiptoes, and he lowered his head. His lips brushed hers lightly, and he pulled back, as if testing her. When she didn't turn away, he released her hands to draw her into his arms and kissed her again, this time for real.

Warmth exploded inside, filling all those places that she didn't realize had been empty until that moment. For the first time in so long, she felt truly cherished, something she hadn't felt since before Darren walked away. No, she hadn't even felt it then. At least not to this extent.

Zack was like a rock, not the type to shy away from the tough things.

Tough things.

The thought was like a splash of cold water. No, she couldn't take what Zack was offering when he had no idea what he was committing to. She pulled back and twisted away.

He dropped his arms. "I'm sorry. I shouldn't have kissed you. I promise it'll never happen again. A relationship with me would be anything but easy. I wouldn't ask that of any woman, and I won't ask that of you."

"What are you talking about?" Granted, she was a little dizzy from that kiss, but she couldn't make any sense of what he'd just said.

"If we moved into a romantic relationship, you wouldn't just be getting me, you'd be taking on William, too. You're great with him, and I appreciate everything you're doing to help him through the loss of his mom. But if you don't feel like you can commit to this for the long haul, especially after everything you've been through, I totally get it."

Her jaw dropped. "Is that what you think?

You're dead wrong. I'd take on William in a heart-beat. He's hurting and angry, but deep down, he's a good kid."

Zack's eyebrows drew together. A range of emotions flitted across his face before sadness settled in his eyes. He released a heavy sigh, his shoulders slouching. "So, it's me."

"No." She rested a hand on his forearm. "Not at all. Trust me, this has nothing to do with you. It's all me."

He cast her a doubt-infused glance. "So you're saying it's not me, it's you."

She winced. How many times over the centuries had that phrase been used when someone just wasn't interested?

She sank onto the trunk of the downed tree. "Please sit with me."

Zack moved closer and sat, a heavy sigh showing his reluctance.

"I told you about losing my mother to cancer. She was forty-three. Two years later, I fought my own battle with the disease. I was nineteen."

"I'm so sorry." He looked at her, his expression moving from sympathy to concern. "I assume the treatment was successful. I mean, it's been ten years, right? You're okay?"

"The treatment was successful. But chemo alone didn't do it. I had to have a hysterectomy." A lump formed in her throat, and she dipped her gaze to the dead leaves on the ground all around her. "I'll never be able to have children."

She forced the words out from somewhere deep inside. They always hurt, but this time they felt razor-sharp, shredding her heart before making it to her lips. When she glanced at Zack again, he looked as if he'd just been kicked in the gut.

"Any man who wants a relationship with me would have to accept the fact that he'll never have children of his own."

Zack nodded slowly. "A lot of women can't have children for one reason or another. That doesn't make you broken or somehow inferior. Adoption is always an option."

Two words sank into her heart, as if shouted through a megaphone—*broken* and *inferior*. She'd struggled with feeling both for the past ten years. Leave it to Zack to be able to zero in on emotions she hadn't shared with anyone, even Kat.

There was an earnestness in his eyes, making her heart twist. Before he recovered from the last blow, she was going to kick him again.

"My mom didn't even see her forty-fourth birthday. She didn't get to attend Lyle's high school graduation. She never even experienced her first gray hair."

Zack put an arm across her shoulders and gave her a little shake. "Just because your mom died of cancer doesn't mean you will. You had it once, ten years ago. What are the chances it'll come back after all this time?"

She clasped her hands together in her lap, eyes fixed on her fidgeting fingers. "Good, actually. Have you ever heard of Lynch Syndrome?"

"No."

"How about someone carrying the cancer gene?"

A heavy silence followed. When she looked up at him, he was studying her, lips pressed together and jaw tight. Yes, he'd heard of it, and his mind was rebelling against the possibility that something so deadly could be hiding inside her.

"Families with Lynch Syndrome have more instances of cancer than expected. It also causes cancers to happen at an earlier age. William already lost his mother. He doesn't need to risk going through the experience a second time."

After several moments of silence, she pushed herself to her feet. "We'd better get what we want and haul it back to the cabin."

There was no need for him to respond to the bombshell she'd just dropped on him. Maybe she should have told him sooner. But that wasn't something to throw out there upon first meeting someone. *Hello, my name is Lauren Hollander, and I carry the cancer gene.*

They headed back, Zack dragging a limb with each hand, and her struggling with one tucked against her side, its end clasped in both hands.

The only sounds that accompanied their trek were the crunch of their footsteps in the dry leaves and the *shhh* of the branches being dragged along the ground. At least now he knew. It really was all her.

When she reached the part of the clearing that Zack had designated as his log-splitting area, she dropped the end of the branch she'd been dragging.

"I'm going to get my water bottle from around back and then go inside. I'll let you know when I have our sandwiches made."

He gave her a sharp nod. He was having a hard time digesting what she'd told him. He would come to grips with it in time. Then they'd fall back into the easy camaraderie of friends.

Just before she rounded the front corner of the cabin, his voice stopped her.

"Lauren?"

She spun to face him. He was holding his phone.

"I'm going to have to charge this. I've got enough juice for one more phone call."

She nodded. Charging the phone would involve a trip to the Mustang. Matt had warned her. The DC port in the Kawasaki no longer worked. "William and I will be safe here with Ranger while you're gone."

She headed behind the cabin and retrieved her water bottle from the stump where she'd placed it earlier. The shortest way inside would be through the back door. But since it led into the bedroom and she didn't know where William was, she walked toward the corner to circle around front.

Repeated sharp cracks of the ax came from the other side of the clearing. Zack was hard at work. He was probably getting some benefit from the physical exertion.

Just before she rounded the corner, heavy footsteps sounded behind her. *William?*

She spun toward the sound. The stocky man who'd attacked her previously was closing on her fast, in spite of the limping gait. A fraction of a second later, he slammed into her. The shriek she emitted came in time with another crack of the ax. A beefy hand over her mouth immediately cut it short. So did the knife at her throat.

"You make a peep, and both you and your boyfriend will be dead." He hissed the words into her ear. "Got that?"

She glanced toward the woods where the other man in her photos was waiting. A cloth bag was hanging from a strap over his shoulder. Fairly flat and measuring about sixteen by twenty inches, it didn't look like something that would carry a weapon.

It didn't matter. The knife was enough to keep her in line.

"Come with us quietly, and no one will get hurt."

She nodded, and he lowered the hand covering her mouth. "That's a good girl."

The knife came away next. She instinctively put a hand to her throat. Though she'd felt the sharp edge of the blade, he hadn't cut her.

"Now go." He rested the point between her shoulder blades, prodding her toward the woods. She obeyed.

The three of them walked single file, the other man in the lead. After they'd covered about a half mile, he stopped. "This is far enough."

"What do you want?" If they simply wanted to kill her, they would have slit her throat behind the cabin.

"You're going to make some pictures disappear." He pulled a laptop from the bag he carried. It was the new one taken from her house.

After commanding her to sit on a log, he handed her the computer. It still had a full charge. Of course, they'd probably seen to that.

"We'd hoped we could do this ourselves, but we were never able to get past the code to unlock your screen. Get in and find those pictures."

Uh-oh. That would be a problem.

While she entered the code, the man moved behind her. She navigated to the picture folder. It was empty, as she knew it would be. Since getting her new computer, she'd uploaded every picture she'd taken directly to the cloud.

"They're not here. I guess I already deleted them."

"You must think we're stupid." He stepped over the log so he was once again standing in front of her. "We knew you had probably put them in online storage. Don't worry. We came prepared." He pulled his phone from his pocket and frowned. "Still no service. Check yours."

The other man did the same. Rouse, if she remembered correctly. That was one of his names, anyway. "None here, either."

The taller man stepped behind her. The next thing she knew, he'd stuffed a gag into her mouth. She whipped her head to the side and lifted a hand to remove it.

Rouse grabbed that wrist and leaned toward her, putting his face inches from hers. "Fight him, and I get the knife back out."

Her gaze dipped to where he'd tucked it into the case hanging from his belt. Why were they gagging her? What did they have planned?

"Go get that phone." The command came from the taller guy.

Rouse nodded, eagerness in his eyes. "We always have a plan B, don't we, boss?" He turned his attention to her. "Good thing we saw you make that call. Your boyfriend's satellite phone's gonna come in real handy."

Lauren's chest clenched. Rouse wouldn't be

able to surprise Zack like they had her. He'd be on high alert, frantically searching for her.

"If he gives you any trouble, shoot him."

The tall man's words sent panic coursing through her. *God, please protect him.*

Rouse patted his hip, making the bulge of a pistol visible. "You got it, Marv."

The taller man flashed a silent warning, obviously unhappy his buddy had used his name. Lauren closed her eyes, desperation overtaking her. The same man who'd shot her brother was headed for the cabin, and she couldn't even warn Zack.

Maybe he didn't realize she was gone. Probably only thirty minutes had passed. He might still be cutting wood, wondering when she was going to announce that sandwiches were ready. If Rouse could take the phone without a struggle, maybe Zack wouldn't get hurt.

God, please let that be the case.

Zack swung the ax down hard. The short log he'd struck split into two halves, one landing on each side of the upright stump he'd been using for the task. After splitting each half into quarters, he placed them on one of his stacks.

Having lived in LA all his life, splitting firewood wasn't something he had much experience with, but over the past few days, he'd developed skills that he'd pit against any Tennessee native.

He bent his arms and twisted side to side, wincing against protesting muscles. He wasn't out of shape. It had been less than three weeks since his last trip to the gym. Splitting wood obviously used different muscle groups from lat pulldowns, rows and reverse flies.

Before leaving LA, he'd done an online search for gyms near Ridgely. The nearest he'd found was in Dyersburg, thirty minutes away. That search was as far as he'd gotten. Once things settled down, he'd pursue it further. Maybe he and William could be workout buddies.

He gathered an armload of firewood and headed for the cabin. What was taking Lauren so long? She'd gone inside a good thirty minutes ago. How long could it take to open a bag of chips, make a few peanut butter and honey sandwiches and lay out some fruit?

He stepped onto the porch, the boards creaking under his feet. After twisting the knob, he pushed the door open the rest of the way with his foot. Once inside, he laid the firewood next to the stove and straightened. William was sitting on the couch playing a game, Ranger lying at his feet. No one moved about the kitchen.

"Where's Lauren?"

William answered without looking up. "She's outside working with you."

"No, she came in a half hour ago to make sandwiches."

"No, she didn't."

"Are you sure?"

William did look up now. Concern had crept into his features. "I'm positive. I've been sitting right here the whole time."

Zack frowned, a lead weight filling his stomach. "Stay inside."

He hit the door at a half run then sailed from the porch to the ground, skipping the two steps.

"Lauren!" He frantically scanned the small clearing, squinting into the tree line and shouting her name as he circled the cabin.

Even as he called, he knew she wouldn't answer. The men had somehow found her and had been waiting for her when she'd walked around back to retrieve her water. More than thirty minutes had passed since then. Why hadn't he checked on her sooner?

He searched the ground for any sign of which way they'd gone. Leaves had been kicked around and scattered, mostly by their own feet as they'd gathered firewood. If there'd been a struggle, it wasn't obvious.

He pulled his phone from his pocket. He'd call 9-1-1 and tell William to stay hidden inside. Then he'd command Ranger to search for her. If she hadn't been taken away in a vehicle, the dog would find her. He only hoped the police would get there quickly.

A breeze rustled the trees and sent dried leaves

swirling around his feet. He pressed the phone icon. His most recent calls came up, Lauren's to Rutherford at the top.

As he tapped to switch to the keypad, there was a different type of sound—a crunch rather than a rustle. He spun to see the stocky man from Lauren's pictures advancing, a heavy limb raised over his head. The next moment, it connected hard with his right temple.

He stumbled sideways as stars exploded across his vision. A high-pitched ring surrounded him, drowning out the rustle of the breeze through the trees. Or maybe the annoying sound was inside his head. The stars faded and darkness rolled in from all sides. He dropped to his knees, and the phone slipped from his hand. Leaves crunched beneath him as he fell forward, facedown.

There was a muffled thud nearby, like a branch hitting the leaf-covered ground. The attacker had dropped his makeshift weapon. Feet crunched through the dead leaves and then stopped next to him. Did the man plan to pick up his phone? Hit him again? Shoot him?

He needed to finish the 9-1-1 call. But his limbs seemed to be filled with lead. No part of his body was willing to follow his brain's commands.

The ringing sound lowered in pitch, the rustle of dried leaves somewhere in the background. Then both faded until they disappeared altogether...

...Zack was floating. No, not floating. The surface at his back was too hard. Where was he? He should open his eyes, but the action required too much effort. He wanted to drift back into that place of oblivion where he'd been moments earlier, but pain stabbing through the side of his head tethered him here. What had happened?

The attack at the cabin rushed back to him with the force of a tidal wave, and his eyes snapped open. Had he blacked out? He must have, because he was no longer facedown. He was on his back, staring up at bare limbs silhouetted against a blue sky. He was moving. Someone was dragging him through the forest. He raised his head to see the backside of his attacker. The man held him by the feet, one boot trapped under each arm. He was strongly favoring his right leg.

Zack lowered his head again, willing the fog in his brain to clear. He needed all his faculties. Both his and Lauren's lives depended on it. Wherever the man was taking him, he couldn't go in weak or restrained.

In one swift motion, he twisted and rolled to the side, keeping his boots pressed against his attacker's rib cage. The man released his feet and threw his arms out in an attempt to catch himself. He stumbled sideways, tripping over a root, and hit the ground with a thud.

Then Zack was on top of him. The man threw a punch toward his face, and Zack leaned to the side, making it a grazing blow. His own fist connected solidly with the man's jaw.

With a roar of anger, the man bucked him off. Zack landed hard on his side, a root digging into his shoulder. When he sprang to his feet, a wave of dizziness washed through him. The ground tilted sideways and rose up to meet him. He crash-landed on one hip.

When he sat up, he was staring into the barrel of a pistol.

TEN

Lauren sat ramrod-straight, heart pounding in her chest. Moments ago, she'd heard tussling and grunting. A roar of anger had followed. Then nothing.

There wasn't anything she could do to protect herself. Besides the gag they'd stuffed into her mouth, Rouse's buddy had taken a coil of rope from the bag that held the laptop and insisted she be tied up. So Rouse had pulled her arms around the small tree at her back and bound her wrists together.

It hadn't taken long to figure out that Marv was the brains of the operation, and Rouse was the brawn. Restraining her, though, hadn't been necessary. It wasn't like she could escape when that pistol could come out at any moment.

Said pistol was now drawn and pointed toward the source of the recent commotion. The man crept in that direction, leaving her alone.

For several tense minutes, she waited. Voices

reached her, both male. Neither was Zack's. Had he been hurt, maybe left for dead?

Less than a minute later, he appeared, both hands raised. Her breath escaped in a rush. He was alive. The other two men appeared right behind him. Not only was Zack alive. He also appeared unhurt.

Rouse didn't. Besides the limp, thanks to Ranger, the left side of his lower jaw was red, as if he'd been hit with something. She hoped it was Zack's fist. They'd obviously been on the ground tussling. Both men had dried leaves clinging to their clothing. William wasn't with them. Had Rouse hurt him somehow?

No, she wouldn't even entertain that thought. Rouse had likely attacked Zack outside. If so, he wouldn't have had any reason to go into the cabin and discover William and Ranger.

By now William would know that she and Zack were gone. He may have even watched Zack being led away. When the men had tried to abduct her from Food Rite, the boy had thought quickly. The old man with the cane had helped, but if it hadn't been for William setting Ranger loose on the guy, she would have already been stuffed into the car by the time the cane-wielding senior had gotten to them.

Marv reached into the bag he'd left lying against a tree and extracted a second coil of rope. "Tie him up."

Rouse slid his pistol into its holster and caught the rope the other man tossed to him. He shoved Zack so hard, he stumbled and cracked his head against a tree. Lauren released an involuntary cry of protest.

When he had Zack tied up in the same way he'd restrained her, he stuck his hand into his pocket and pulled out a phone.

"You'll have to work fast." He handed the item to his partner. "His stupid phone's almost dead."

With the last statement, he gave Zack an angry kick in the side. Zack groaned and Lauren flinched. For a brief moment, Rouse's face registered pain, too. But he wasn't letting the damage Ranger had done to the back of his leg hinder him from releasing his anger on Zack. She could guess what had happened. Zack had fought him, had even gotten in a punch to the jaw.

Things were likely to get ugly as the afternoon progressed. But the other guy wouldn't let him hurt them. He needed them. He needed Zack's phone, and he needed her to access her cloud storage and delete the photos she'd taken in the park.

But once the men had what they wanted, there'd be no reason to keep them alive. Tied to trees somewhere deep in the woods, escape would be impossible, and the likelihood of someone stumbling across them was nil.

God, please send help.

Marv fiddled with the phone and then laid her

laptop on the ground next to her. His gaze shifted to his partner. "Untie her and remove the gag."

As Rouse did what he was instructed, Marv continued. "I've turned on the mobile hot spot. Get into your cloud storage and find those pictures. Make it fast."

Once free of the gag, Lauren nodded. "I'll try, but it might take some time."

Maybe she could stall until the phone went dead. The longer she could delay, the greater the chances that help would arrive before it was too late. She hadn't known William long, but she knew him well enough to believe he wouldn't sit in the cabin and wait for help to come to them. He'd go in search of that help.

The man frowned and crossed his arms. "Why would it take time?"

"My book of password hints is at home. I use three basic passwords, with slightly different variations for each account."

He heaved a sigh. "Just hurry. If this phone goes dead before you get those pictures deleted, things won't be pleasant for you or your boyfriend."

She pressed her lips together. For her, the words were an empty threat. Until she deleted those pictures, they needed her. But they didn't need Zack. They already had what they wanted from him. She cast him a sideways glance, and he gave her an almost imperceptible shake of his head.

What did that mean? Did he want her to hurry and give them what they wanted? Or did he want her to stretch it out as long as possible? She'd go with the latter.

She typed in a user name and password. A message came up saying that one or the other was incorrect. She tried a second time with the same result.

After the fourth time, he nudged her leg with one foot. "Click to change the password. I'm sure you can get into your email."

Her heart fell. Yes, she could get to her Gmail account with a single click. Her login information was saved. How much charge was left on the phone? How much longer would the battery last before it went dead?

She typed "yahoo.com" into the URL bar. Maybe after several unsuccessful attempts, she would try Outlook.

No, it would never work. Rouse might fall for it, but his buddy wouldn't.

"How often do you check your email? Daily? A few times a week?"

She looked up at the taller man. He hadn't asked the question to get an answer. He'd been making a point. He shifted his gaze to where Zack sat on the ground, arms tied behind his back. Then he looked at his accomplice and dipped his head. An eager grin spread across the man's face.

Lauren held up a hand. "No—"

It was too late. Rouse's boot slammed into Zack's side with even more force than it had the first time. A scream escaped before Zack pressed his lips together, face contorted in pain.

Lauren's heart twisted. She couldn't do this. She couldn't keep stalling while the men hurt Zack.

"Maybe I set it up with my Gmail account."

The tall man patted her shoulder. "Now that's a good girl."

Her hands shook as she typed her email provider into the URL bar. Her inbox displayed instantly, the password reset email at the top. She was out of options. She could work slowly, but soon there'd be no more ways to delay the inevitable.

She opened the email and looked at the password reset code. Instead of copying and pasting the eight-digit number, she clicked back and forth a few times, entering two digits at a time.

Soon two rectangular boxes appeared, with instructions to enter and reenter her new password. She thought for several moments, lower lip pulled between her teeth. The password wouldn't matter, because once the men had what they wanted, she and Zack would be dead. No, this was her last opportunity to stall, even briefly.

"Come on, pick something. You can change it later."

She typed her new password into the first space. When she typed it again, she transposed two characters. Upon seeing the error message, the man stuffed the phone into his back pocket and snatched the laptop from her.

After putting the computer next to her, he dropped to one knee, hands on the keyboard. He was going to choose a password himself. He'd be into her cloud storage in moments. With all her folders labeled by date and location, it wouldn't take him any time to find what he was looking for.

She glanced at the rectangular bulge in his back pocket. *Come on, die already.*

A soft buzz sounded, and he straightened suddenly. He withdrew the phone and stared at the screen. Anger flashed across his features. She didn't need to see what he held to know what had happened. The phone had died.

Thank You, Lord.

She looked up at him, keeping her expression neutral. "What's wrong?"

When he didn't respond, she turned the computer toward her and looked at the lower right corner of the screen. The curved lines showing the strength of the signal had disappeared, giving way to the globe vector icon with a line through it. "We lost the internet."

"Of course we did, thanks to your stalling." His anger was much more controlled than what his buddy had displayed.

He passed off the phone. "Take this back to the cabin and get it charged."

Panic flashed in Zack's eyes. "The charger's not there." His breathing was rapid and shallow. He likely had some cracked ribs. "There's no power at the cabin. We knew that before we came. I only have the car charger. It's plugged in to the lighter port on my dash." He sucked in some more panting breaths and looked up at Rouse. "If you walk back to the cabin with me, I can take you there in the Kawasaki."

Rouse gave a derisive snort. "You think we're stupid or something?"

He clenched both hands into fists, and Lauren's heart almost stopped. He was going to hurt Zack again.

Marv held up a hand. "That's enough. Take his keys. Make sure you've got one for both the car and the four-wheeler."

Rouse reached into Zack's right front pocket and pulled out one set of keys. The other pocket was empty.

He held up the ring. "Both keys are on here?"

"They are." Zack paused. "How are you going to find the car?"

"You underestimate us." It was Marv who spoke. "Finding your car was easy. Figuring out where you were hiding took us almost three days."

After stuffing the keys and phone into his

pockets, Rouse headed away from them at a limping jog.

Lauren looked over at Zack. His eyebrows were drawn together, and his jaw was tight. He was afraid. He no longer had just the two of them to worry about. Now William was in imminent danger.

If the boy had gone to get help, he'd be on foot. He couldn't have taken the Mule, because Zack had the key. The boy and dog were likely hurrying down the overgrown drive, making their way to the gravel roads that would eventually take them to the highway.

If William heard the off-road vehicle approaching, would he veer into the woods and hide until he knew for sure who was driving it?

Or would he just assume it was Zack and try to flag him down?

"That's the last one."

Zack watched as Lauren handed her laptop to the taller man. After disappearing for an hour, Rouse had come back claiming he had the phone charged at thirty percent. It had been enough for what the men had wanted her to do.

"How do I know you don't have the photos saved somewhere else?"

"I already took you to my pictures folder. You've seen they're not saved to my computer."

"What about other cloud storage?"

"Besides the extra work, why would I pay for two separate services?"

Her response seemed to satisfy him. He slid the laptop back into the bag. Lauren had stalled as long as she could. Zack admired her for her efforts. He didn't even fault her for what she'd done that had earned him some probable cracked ribs.

While she'd been stalling, he'd been working on plans of his own. When Rouse had forced his arms around the tree behind him, Zack had pressed his palms together, leaving a gap between his wrists. Though the rope wasn't tied as tightly as it could have been, working one hand free hadn't been as easy as he'd hoped. All he'd accomplished so far was creating rope burns on the back of his left hand.

Lauren broke the silence. "I've given you what you wanted. Now let us go."

The taller man crossed his arms. "Who are you working for?"

"What are you talking about?"

"Who sent you to the park to take those pictures? Did Lyle set it up?"

At the mention of her brother's name, pain flashed across her features. "I didn't even know he was involved with you."

"He's *been* involved with us. He thought he could get out by leaving Memphis. That's not how it works. There's only one way out—in a box. He didn't like that option, so we gave him a chance to prove his loyalty. He balked a little at robbing you but finally agreed. Taking care of Kerman, though, was another story. He needed a little persuasion for that, something you would have provided quite well."

Zack silently willed Lauren to keep the man talking. This couldn't be the end. What would happen to William if he and Lauren didn't return?

Where was he now? Since Rouse didn't say he'd come across anyone, he likely hadn't encountered William. Had the boy gone to get help, or was he hunkered down in the cabin, hoping he or Lauren would somehow manage to escape and return?

The latter didn't sound like his nephew. He'd proven that at Food Rite. No, if it came down to it, William would try to find help. He was a smart kid. He was also caring. That care and concern just had a hard time leaking out through all the grief and anger. *God, please give us a chance to get close.*

Zack looked at Lauren. Her tone was firm and persuasive. "Look, Lyle's gone, and I'm no threat. I have no idea what you do, and I don't care. Just let us go. You can return to your activities, and you'll never see or hear from us again."

"You know we can't do that. We have no idea what your brother told you. For all we know, you could have names and information that could bring down the whole organization."

"If that was true, why do you think he came into my store in a ski mask and used that phony Spanish accent? You know how I learned it was him? From law enforcement. Lyle never told me anything."

He thought for a moment. "I believe you."

"So you'll let us go?"

He shook his head. "You sealed your fate when you took those pictures."

"The pictures don't prove anything," she said. "Neither does my seeing you together in the park, since I have no idea what you discussed."

"We're not taking any chances. We don't leave loose ends."

"Then let Zack go. He doesn't have anything to do with this. He left California just two weeks ago. He's never even met Lyle."

"He's a loose end by association."

The man looked at his accomplice. Zack's pulse went into high gear. This was it. *God, please help me.* If he could just wiggle one hand free. He rotated his left hand side to side as he pulled, trying to keep the strain from showing on his face.

"There's something you might want to know." He managed to keep his voice level, even though his heart was pounding in his throat. He now had both men's attention, but he wouldn't stop trying to get free. As he spoke, he cupped his hands and worked the right one over the back of the left. It was wet. He'd worn away enough skin that he was bleeding.

"Those photos Lauren deleted have already been turned over to the police." He shifted his gaze to the shorter guy. "They've already identified you. One of your aliases is Edwin Rouse. They know others, too."

The man's nostrils flared. Zack had hit a nerve. He looked at the other man again. "The police are still working on identifying you. You kill us, and they're going to work that much harder."

Concern flashed across the man's features. Zack continued twisting his hand back and forth. It was working. The rope was around the knuckles of his left hand.

Rouse heaved a sigh. "You're not buying that, are you? Come on, let's get this over with." He put his hand on the holster at his side, his fingers twitching with anticipation. "I wanna be outta here before dark and sleeping in a nice warm bed tonight."

The taller man gave a sharp nod. "You're right."

Rouse's lips curved upward in an eager grin and he pulled the pistol from its holster. The man truly got some sick satisfaction from killing. As he raised the pistol, Zack's left hand suddenly slid free.

Relief washed through him, but hopelessness immediately stamped it out. With that pistol pointed at his head, he'd be dead before he could rise from the ground.

The man looked back at his partner without lowering the weapon. "After we shoot 'em, are we just gonna leave 'em here for the wild animals?"

"We're sure not hauling them back to Memphis."

"Bummer." He narrowed his eyes at Zack. "I'd like to run this one through the big man's mulcher."

"It's not a mulcher. It's a tire rasper."

"Whatever."

The taller man held up a hand, body suddenly rigid. "Wait." He'd lowered his voice to a whisper. "Did you hear that?"

"I didn't hear nothing but the wind." His voice wasn't lowered. He obviously didn't see the need for caution that his accomplice did.

The other man still had his hand up. He pulled his weapon from its holster, but instead of pointing it at any of them, he spun to face in the direction they'd come from early that afternoon.

Zack strained to hear above the rustle of the leaves. The wind had picked up and was now a steady *shhh*, so loud and constant that it resembled a heavy rain shower. Was there also the occasional soft crunch of dried leaves?

Suddenly, something was barreling toward them through the woods, not even trying to use stealth. Rouse spun, his weapon expelling a round. Whether intentional or not, Zack couldn't guess.

But he wouldn't waste the unexpected distraction. He sprang to his feet and rammed into the guy from behind. As he tumbled forward, the gun fell from his hand. He sprawled facedown in the leaves, the weapon two feet out of his reach.

Zack threw himself on top of him, the impact sending excruciating pain shooting through his side. The man bucked him off and lunged toward where the pistol lay.

As Rouse's left hand closed around the barrel, Zack dove over him and gripped the handle. For several moments, they wrestled for possession of the weapon. Somewhere nearby, heavy footsteps seemed to come from all directions.

Suddenly, Ranger charged toward them, his eyes on Zack. Then the brown gaze landed on Rouse, and the dog skidded to a stop not ten feet away. Tension rippled through his body. He bared his teeth and growled.

The man froze briefly before jamming his elbow into Zack's side. For the third time, pain exploded through his rib cage, and he lost his grip on the gun. The man grabbed the handle with his other hand and pointed the weapon at Ranger.

"Call your dog off, or I'll shoot him."

Before Zack could respond, a commanding male voice came from nearby. "Drop your weapons and put your hands up. You're surrounded."

Zack looked up to see a half dozen law enforcement personnel moving toward them, pistols drawn. Lauren was standing a few feet from him with a stick raised over her head.

For several tense moments, no one moved. Then the taller man bent to lay his weapon on the ground and slowly raised his hands.

Zack stood and raised his hands, too. Until all those armed law enforcement guys knew for sure who the bad guys were, he wasn't about to make any sudden moves.

One of the police officers moved closer, weapon trained on the man still on the ground. "Drop the gun. Now."

Unlike his accomplice, he hadn't laid down his weapon. His gaze met the officer's, and he lay unmoving, as if deciding what course of action to take.

Finally, he released the weapon and rose. His hands went up slowly. When they reached shoulder height, he suddenly spun and ran, sheer adrenaline making the limp less pronounced than it had been. Ranger released a bark that dissolved into a fierce growl and shot off after the man.

"Ranger!"

Rouse was no longer armed, but the dog could still get hurt. Both man and dog disappeared, three officers in pursuit. Seconds later, an agonized scream echoed through the woods.

Zack smiled. The dog had caught his prey.

Ranger wasn't aggressive. He wasn't trained as a guard dog, but after seeing this man attack two of his favorite people, he was out for blood.

Zack looked around him. Two officers were cuffing the taller man and reading him his rights. A third was talking softly with Lauren.

Where was William? Why hadn't he been with Ranger? Had the man found him when he'd gone to charge the phone and hurt him? No, Ranger wouldn't have led the police to them on his own. Would he?

Zack looked frantically around, concern morphing to panic. "William? William!"

Rustling sounded a short distance away, growing rapidly louder. Someone or something was charging toward him.

William appeared seconds later, running at full speed. He didn't slow down. He hit Zack with the force of a wrecking ball, knocking him backward several feet. The boy's arms went around his rib cage and he squeezed him with every bit of strength in his young body.

Zack closed his eyes and clenched his jaw against pain that held him in a steel vise. No way was he going to interrupt this moment. There was no telling when, if ever, he'd get another hug from his nephew.

Movement behind him drew both his and William's attention. The boy dropped his arms and stepped away as Zack turned. The officers were leading a handcuffed Rouse toward them, Ranger trotting behind. The dog had apparently bitten him in the left leg this time, because he was having trouble walking, his gait resembling that of someone walking on hot coals.

When Zack looked back at William, the boy's eyes were moist.

"The police officers told me and Ranger to stay back until they had everything under control. I tried to hold on to Ranger, but he took off to get to you."

One of the officers approached. He put a hand on William's shoulder, but his gaze was on Zack.

"You have an amazing young man here. When he couldn't find you, he figured you were in trouble and went to get help. Made it all the way to Highway 100 and flagged someone down. The motorist stayed with him until we arrived. Your boy told us what happened and led us to the cabin. Your dog led us the rest of the way."

Zack smiled, pride swelling inside. "You're right. He *is* amazing." He looked down at his nephew. "You know, you saved our lives today."

William nodded, but his gaze was fixed somewhere beyond Zack, a look of concentration on his face. "Does that mean you'll get me a new video game console?"

Zack laughed. Just like William to see how he could use today's events as a bargaining chip. "Maybe. But I was thinking about a snazzy new rod and reel and a gym membership. I need a fishing partner and a workout buddy. You up for the job?"

Enthusiasm filled his eyes. "Yeah! But I still want the video game console."

Zack gave him a playful shake. "We'll see what we can do."

"Good." He looked at the two men the officers were preparing to march out. "When me and Ranger were going to get help, we heard the four-wheeler coming. I was hoping it was you, but I was afraid it was the bad guys. So we ran away from the trail and hid in the woods till they passed. Sure enough, it was him."

He pointed at Rouse who turned to stare daggers at them. Zack hoped the authorities would hold him for a long time.

Lauren approached them. The officer was apparently finished with her. Zack extended an arm, ready to pull her into a hug. They'd both come so close to dying today.

William got there first, wrapping both arms around Lauren's shoulders. Yep, his own hug would have to wait.

The officer approached him, and Zack relayed everything that had happened from the time that he'd realized Lauren was gone. When he'd finished, the officer nodded. "You probably should go to the emergency room and get checked out. At least urgent care."

"I'll be all right." The pain was just a dull ache. Unless he got hugged. Or moved. Or tried to breathe. Okay, maybe he should take the officer's advice.

Soon, all eleven of them plus Ranger were hiking through the woods toward civilization. Lauren spoke to the officer nearest them. "Where are your cruisers parked?"

"We're lined up at the edge of Cagle Trail."

"You're welcome to take the Mule. It won't accommodate all of you, but if two ride in the bed, you can fit four of you plus the two suspects."

"We might take you up on that."

"Zack and I will follow so we can drive it back to the cabin and load up our stuff."

Lauren slowed her pace, allowing some space between them and the others. William walked behind the officers, Ranger trotting next to him.

Zack put his arm around her and she looked up at him. "How did they find us?"

"Something led them to my car. It had to have been a tracking device."

"But you and Danny checked."

"We must have missed it. We checked the wheel wells, bumpers, the usual places. They couldn't have gotten to the interior, because I always keep my car locked with the alarm set. Maybe they used your duct tape idea and stuck it somewhere up in the engine compartment."

"We'll definitely want to get rid of it." She

paused. "I can't believe it's over. When you sprang up and tackled Rouse, I thought I was seeing things. How did you get your hands untied?"

"I didn't." He lifted his other arm and showed her the back of his hand. It was raw in places and caked with dried blood.

"Ouch."

"It took me a while, but I finally managed to pull that hand free."

"I gave the cops the guys' names. The taller guy's name is Marv."

"How did you learn that?"

"His buddy slipped. He wasn't too happy about it."

"So where is your notebook with all your password hints?"

She grinned. "I don't have one. All those password hints are on my computer in a Word doc titled 'Lauren's Brain.'"

He matched her smile. "Sneaky."

"Hey, my stalling bought us the time we needed. If your phone hadn't gone dead, those guys would have shot us long before the police arrived."

"I know. I was doing some serious praying."

She nodded. "So was I."

He lowered his voice. "For the past couple of hours, I've been doing some serious thinking, too."

"Oh?"

"There's nothing like facing your own mortality to make you realize what's truly important."

She waited for him to continue, and he lowered his voice even further. "The conversation we had, when you told me you couldn't have children, it felt like a blow. I've always planned to have a kid or two. But I've got William. He's enough for me. There's always the possibility of adoption, too."

"What about the other situation?"

"Life is full of uncertainty."

Lauren smiled. "Kat told me exactly the same thing."

He lifted his brows. "Were you two talking about me?"

Her smile turned sheepish. "Sort of. I was giving her the reasons why we couldn't be more than friends, and she was debunking all of them."

"A true friend." He drew in a deep breath. "Control has always been important to me."

She grinned. "I've gathered that."

"It's taken some hard lessons, but I'm gradually learning that I don't need to be in control all the time, because God is." He stopped and turned her to face him. "Your gentle touch is just what William needs. And it's exactly what I need. Kat is right. Life is full of uncertainty. But there's one thing I know without a doubt. I don't want to try living mine without you."

She looped her arms around his neck and

pulled him closer. When he dipped his head, she rose up on her tiptoes to meet him halfway.

His lips met hers, and she tightened her embrace. This kiss was every bit as powerful as the first one. But this time, she was returning his affections without reservation.

"Ewww."

Zack broke contact to see that William had turned around and was watching them.

Maybe he thought what he'd witnessed was gross. That was typical for someone his age.

The kid was going to have to get used to displays of affection, because he had no intention of hiding what he felt for Lauren.

Regardless of William's comment, Zack was pretty sure that wasn't going to be a problem.

Because the way one side of the kid's mouth curved up announced his approval.

EPILOGUE

Lauren strolled out onto the public fishing pier at Reelfoot Lake State Park. A gust of wind swept across the water, and she wrapped her jacket more tightly around her.

On either side of the pier, bald cypress trees rose from the surface of the lake, their wide bases punctuated by short, knobby spires. A few months ago, green had given way to tan, cinnamon and fiery orange along the droopy limbs before the needly leaves had fallen away altogether.

At the end of the pier, William stood next to Zack, both wearing windbreakers, a tackle box between them. Zack slowly reeled in his line while William baited a hook. The fishing pole that it dangled from had been a gift, given by his uncle a few days after the incident at the cabin.

In the three months since then, William had become a different kid. He'd developed several close friendships with boys in the church youth group. One of them was with him today. Noah was the pastor's nephew and had been one of the kids to welcome William when he'd visited the first time.

Lauren was only halfway down the pier when her phone rang. She slid it from her back pocket and looked at the screen. It was Danny. It had been a while since she'd heard from him.

She turned and headed back up the pier. "What's up?"

"Thought you might be interested in some Memphis news."

"I am, especially if it involves arrests."

So far, the only arrests made in her and Zack's abductions and the deaths of Samuel and Beverly Kerman had been the two men they'd apprehended in the woods near the cabin. They hadn't been acting on their own, but neither of them would talk.

Their original lead hadn't panned out. The developer who'd requested the zoning variance had no connections with either of the men they'd arrested. After the commissioner's death, the others had turned down the request, so the apartment plans had been scrapped.

"Yeah, it involves arrests, about a dozen of them."

Lauren stepped off the pier. She'd just about given up on seeing the men responsible for Lyle's death brought to justice.

Danny continued. "Your tire rasper lead is

what got everyone headed in the right direction. The developer has his hands in several businesses, but tire recycling isn't one of them. So authorities were investigating the handful of businesses like that in the area. Turns out one of those companies is owned by a George Kerman."

"Same last name as the commissioner."

"Yep. It's not a common name, so they delved a little deeper. Turns out he and Samuel were cousins."

She stepped off the sidewalk and headed toward the pavilion a short distance away. "So why did he want him dead?"

"Good ol' George was using his tire recycling business as a front for drug running. Not only did Samuel find out about it, his son OD'd on some of George's product. Almost died. Samuel and his wife were furious and swore they'd make him pay."

"George Kerman admitted this?"

"Only when the detectives presented him with what they'd already learned from the kid."

Wow, no wonder it had taken them so long to put all the pieces together. "So, he's been charged with drug running *and* murder?"

"Yep, just yesterday. It took that long to definitively link him to the two men who kidnapped you and Zack. The other arrests are people both up and down his supply chain."

Lauren leaned against one of the pavilion's

posts and released a sigh. So these were the guys Lyle had been hooked up with in Memphis. It was finally over. Everyone involved would pay for their crimes. Eventually, she and Zack would have to testify against Rouse and his partner. At least they were alive to do it, unlike Samuel and Beverly Kerman.

Lauren thanked him and headed down the pier. Two months ago, she'd had a memorial service for Lyle. It had been well-attended. Some had come to pay their final respects to her brother, but most of them were there to support her.

When she reached the end of the dock, she ran a hand across Zack's back. "Catching anything?"

He looked at her over one shoulder. "Cold."

She laughed. The February day had started out sunny but cool. Now the wind had picked up and the sun was hiding behind the clouds.

"So our planned fish fry tonight is likely to turn into a taco bar."

Zack bumped her with one hip. "You're not showing much confidence in our fishing skills. The afternoon is still young."

"In the meantime, there's a picnic table back there with a cooler on top filled with ham and cheese sandwiches, fruit and drinks. A bag with a couple of packages of chips, too. There might even be some homemade chocolate-chip cook-ies somewhere, too."

William turned around with an eager grin. If

she ever needed to bribe him, she knew exactly what it would take.

Zack nodded. "That sounds good. Noah, William, you guys ready for some lunch?"

They both answered in the affirmative and reeled in their lines. When they had the hooks secured, they walked back up the pier. Lauren followed, Zack next to her.

She looked up at him. "When we're done eating, if it's too uncomfortable standing on the dock, I've got the two Frisbees in your trunk."

"I'll see what the boys want to do."

If they chose not to play, that would be okay. Fishing was an activity Zack enjoyed with William, and she hadn't wanted to intrude on their time together. So she'd left them on the pier while she'd walked around the park taking pictures.

Besides, fishing wasn't her favorite activity. She didn't like to bait the hook, unless she was using a lure. If she actually caught something, she cringed trying to remove the hook from its mouth. And cleaning what she happened to catch made her gag.

Instead, she had her own activities that she enjoyed with William, one of which was playing video games. That was something else Zack had bought for him—a gaming console that could accommodate anywhere from one to four players. Sometimes all three of them played, and a few times, Zack had invited a friend over, making it four. Often, though, it was just the two of them while Zack was at work. Somehow, playing games with William made her feel closer to Lyle.

Before being kidnapped and taken into the woods, she'd been unable to fully convince herself that her brother hadn't been conning her. That had changed with the one man's words. *He thought he could get out by leaving Memphis. It doesn't work that way.*

Lyle hadn't gone back to a life of crime. At least, not by choice. The man's words had confirmed it. He'd been forced to do things he hadn't wanted to do. And she was the threat they'd held over him.

Lauren stepped down off the pier and made her way to the table. She'd chosen one with no shade. That decision wasn't doing a lot of good at the moment, but hopefully the sun would make an appearance while they ate.

Lauren lifted the strap over her head and laid the camera on the table. After sliding onto the wooden bench opposite her, William pulled a sandwich from the cooler and handed it to Noah. His gaze flicked past his friend to settle on the pavilion about thirty feet away, and his eyes suddenly widened.

"This is the picture."

Zack took a seat beside Lauren. "What picture?"

She knew exactly what picture. She'd seen

the boy studying it so many times. Something about it obviously spoke to him. Maybe it was the thought that the two people with her in that photo had died, but she was still remembering them and holding them close to her heart.

William looked at his uncle. "The picture at Lauren's house." He shifted his attention to her. "When we're done eating lunch, can we do a picture like that? Maybe you could show Noah how to work your camera."

Her heart twisted. He'd lost his mother and, probably without even realizing it, he was afraid of losing the other two most important people in his life. Was he hoping to memorialize them just as she had memorialized her mother and brother?

"Sure. It'll be easy." If she put the settings on automatic, it would be point and click.

After leaving the cabin the day the men were arrested, she and Zack had discussed how much to tell William. They'd decided to keep it all from him—her struggle with cancer, her hysterectomy and the possibility of the cancer returning. She was glad now that they had.

Once the food was distributed, Zack offered a prayer of thanks. Noah and William finished their sandwiches, bananas and chips in record time. For William, that was always the case whenever cookies were involved. Apparently, Noah was the same way.

William turned to his friend. "Wanna throw the Frisbee?"

"Yeah, sure."

Zack handed William his keys. "Don't forget to bring them back."

Both boys shot off toward where he'd parked. When they returned a minute later, William held the orange disk in one hand and the keys in the other. Soon, Lauren and Zack were alone.

When they'd finished their lunch, Zack put their trash in a nearby container.

"Are you wanting to get some more fishing in?"

"I think I'd rather walk a pretty lady around the park."

She smiled. She loved this man. Theirs hadn't been a typical courtship. Most of their "dates" had included a thirteen-year-old who made as good of a chaperone as any proper older woman ever had. If Zack so much as kissed her, the boy just about had a conniption. But she wouldn't change a thing.

After putting the cooler in the car, they strolled hand in hand along the concrete paths that snaked through the park.

"While you were at work yesterday, I picked William up from school, and we checked the construction progress. David was there. He said they passed the plumbing and electrical inspections and plan to have everything dried in next week."

"Sounds like they're ahead of their original estimates."

"They are. We may be only six weeks away from getting the certificate of occupancy. If you want, you guys will actually be able to move back into a brand-new apartment by mid-spring."

Two months ago, Zack had found a place to rent on a month-to-month basis. Mostly, they just slept there. After dropping William off at school in the morning, he and Ranger usually hung out at her place until he left for his shift.

More often than not, instead of having William ride the bus home, Lauren picked him up from school and kept him with her and Ranger until bedtime. Watching the changes in the boy as he'd healed and matured had encouraged her.

Zack hadn't dropped any hints that he wanted to cool things, but he hadn't brought up the subject of marriage, either. Of course, only three months had passed since they'd agreed to take their relationship beyond friendship. Some courtships lasted for years.

Besides, what was the rush? Granted, she was almost thirty, and Zack was a couple of years past, but it wasn't like her biological clock was ticking. Its springs had sprung and those gears had stopped working a decade ago.

Zack pulled her off the concrete path and led her toward a small stand of trees. Once there, he stopped and drew her into his arms. "Do you have any idea how much I love you?"

"If it's anywhere near as much as I love you, I think I do."

And that was her hurry. She loved this man more than she'd ever loved anyone and knew, beyond a doubt, that she wanted to spend the rest of her life making him happy, however long that might be.

The problem was, the longer he waited to make that commitment, the stronger the unfounded fear that he'd decide he couldn't do it after all and would walk away just like Darren had.

Zack pressed his lips together. Something seemed off. Was he nervous? Uneasy? Maybe just distracted.

"I'm sure the apartment is going to be beautiful when it's finished, but I don't think I want to live there."

"You don't?" She swallowed hard. Was he planning to leave the area?

No, he and Ranger had just joined Tennessee Search and Rescue as volunteers. R&K had taken him back after his time at the cabin, plus they'd given him another three weeks for his cracked ribs to begin to heal. He believed they were happy with his performance. His job was secure.

Maybe he wanted more space and planned to use the down payment he'd saved to get a place of his own. Right there in Ridgely. Or no farther away than Tiptonville. She held her breath, waiting for him to speak.

"I'm thinking about something a little more suitable for a family of three and one fairly large dog."

A cautious hope pushed aside a little of her uneasiness. "A family of three?"

"Yep." After releasing her, he slipped a hand into his pocket and pulled out a small velvet box. When he raised the hinged lid, a large solitaire rose from a gold band, four small marquise diamonds circling it.

"Lauren, will you marry me?"

Her jaw dropped, and she snapped it shut again, a large smile spreading across her cheeks. She threw both arms around his neck. "Yes, I'll marry you."

He returned her hug and then disentangled himself from her arms to slide the ring on her finger.

She held out her hand, palm down, admiring the ring, its large diamond sparkling in a stray shaft of sunlight. "It's beautiful."

This was the second engagement ring to grace her finger. This one would stay. She had no doubt.

She looked up at him. "How do you think William will feel about this?"

"Thrilled." He grinned. "He helped me pick out the ring."

"How did you pull that off?"

"Remember when we did our guys' night out last weekend?"

"You said you went to a movie."

"We did. We also went to Rogers Jewelers in Dyersburg."

She tilted her head. "So you've been holding on to this for a week. What took you so long?"

"I was looking for the perfect time and place. Then I decided that anywhere is a good place to ask you to be my wife. Knowing how special this park is to you, I figured I'd propose here."

"You're right. This is perfect." She wrapped her arms around him and pressed a kiss to his mouth. "You realize, you just did business with my competitor."

"I know. But it would have been a little weird for me to offer you something from your safe-deposit box."

She grinned. "You have a point."

He pulled her close again, and she rested her cheek against his chest. Her future looked so bright. In another two months, her store would be open for business. After resigning herself to the fact that she would never have a child of her own to raise and nurture, she had gotten William.

And after feeling for years that she had a heart full of love but no one to share it with, God had brought Zack almost two thousand miles and plunked him right down in the center of her life.

Her heart was so full. *Broken* and *inferior* were

far in the past, all thanks to Zack. He had a way of making her feel like a million bucks.

She silently vowed to spend the rest of her life being as much of a blessing to William and Zack as they'd been to her.

* * * * *

If you enjoyed this story by Carol J. Post,
check out other books by this author.
Available now from Love Inspired Suspense!
Discover more at LoveInspired.com.

Dear Reader,

I hope you've enjoyed Lauren and Zack's story. They were fun characters for me to write. Zack hadn't met a challenge he couldn't overcome... until he became responsible for his grieving nephew and had to accept that, no matter how he wished otherwise, some things were out of his control. Lauren was dealing with her own traumas, so it was fun making these three broken people a family. Through all the life changes, they learned that we can make our plans, but it's God who directs our steps, and He really does make all things work together for the good of those who love Him.

May God richly bless you in all you do.

Love in Christ,
Carol J. Post

Get up to 4 Free Books!

**We'll send you 2 free books from each series you try
PLUS a free Mystery Gift.**

FREE
Value Over
$25

Both the **Love Inspired®** and **Love Inspired® Suspense** series feature compelling
novels filled with inspirational romance, faith, forgiveness and hope.

YES! Please send me 2 FREE novels from the Love Inspired or Love Inspired Suspense series
and my FREE gift (gift is worth about $10 retail). After receiving them, if I don't wish to receive
any more books, I can return the shipping statement marked "cancel." If I don't cancel, I will
receive 6 brand-new Love Inspired Larger-Print books or Love Inspired Suspense Larger-
Print books every month and be billed just $7.19 each in the U.S. or $7.99 each in Canada.
That is a savings of 20% off the cover price. It's quite a bargain! Shipping and handling is
just 50¢ per book in the U.S. and $1.25 per book in Canada.* I understand that accepting
the 2 free books and gift places me under no obligation to buy anything. I can always return
a shipment and cancel at any time by calling the number below. The free books and gift are
mine to keep no matter what I decide.

Choose one: ☐ **Love Inspired**   ☐ **Love Inspired**   ☐ **Or Try Both!**
               Larger-Print   **Suspense**   (122/322 & 107/307 BPA G36Z)
               (122/322 BPA G36Y)   **Larger-Print**
                                           (107/307 BPA G36Y)

Name (please print)

Address   Apt. #

City   State/Province   Zip/Postal Code

Email: Please check this box ☐ if you would like to receive newsletters and promotional emails from Harlequin Enterprises ULC and its affiliates.
You can unsubscribe anytime.

Mail to the Harlequin Reader Service:
IN U.S.A.: P.O. Box 1341, Buffalo, NY 14240-8531
IN CANADA: P.O. Box 603, Fort Erie, Ontario L2A 5X3

Want to explore our other series or interested in ebooks? Visit www.ReaderService.com or call 1-800-873-8635.